lessons learned

je rowney

the lessons of a student midwife

BOOK THREE

Also by this author:

Charcoal
Derelict
Ghosted
I Can't Sleep

THE LESSONS OF A STUDENT MIDWIFE SERIES:

Life Lessons
Love Lessons
Lessons Learned

Chapter One

I went back to visit my mum a few times over the summer break, but for the most part I stayed at Tangiers Court with Zoe, Luke and Carl.

Carl.

My boyfriend.

I thought it was too soon to spend the whole summer with him, but the more time I spent at home with Mum, the more I wanted to be with him.

It felt strange, at first, being in Tangiers Court, and then being in the town, after lectures had finished and there were no other students around. I went onto campus, just out of curiosity, and the squares were dotted with seagulls and pigeons fighting over the last scraps that had been left behind. Apart from that, there was an unusual, eerie silence. When you're used to seeing a place filled with life and noise and chaos, visiting when all of that has left is quite an experience.

I can't believe how much has changed since I started university. I'm about to begin my third and final year as a student midwife; I'm a senior student at last, but I'm not sure I'm ready for it. I've spent the past two years living at Tangiers Court. It's had its ups and downs, but mostly it has been great, living with my best friend, and training for my dream job.

When you suffer from anxiety as I do, there's always some degree of underlying stress, but this year the pressure is really going to be on. I have a practice document (my PAD) that needs to be signed off. To qualify as a midwife, I need to carry out a certain number of deliveries, antenatal and postnatal checks, and other midwifery duties, and have a midwife sign my checklist. I also need to pass the rest of my modules, of course. The academic and the clinical elements are equally as important as each other. This year, I need to complete a research project on my own subject choice. I think I already know what I want to focus on, but lectures are a few days away. I'll wait and see what the module leader tells us.

Then there's Carl.

I actually have a boyfriend.

It's not what I planned, and it's not what I

expected, but things happened gradually between us and now it's official. So now there's Zoe and Luke, me and Carl, all living here together. Even though it's not what I'd planned, this is pretty much everything I ever wanted. In a year's time, I will be starting work as a midwife; everything is working out perfectly.

There's a voice from behind me.

"You are coming out with me tonight?"

Carl loops his arms around me unexpectedly, making me jump slightly.

I don't want to say no. I don't want to be the boring one that never goes anywhere or does anything. If it were down to me, we would stay at home with Zoe and Luke, watch television, chat and all have a laugh together. Carl is far more sociable than I am. It's the first night of freshers' week, and even though we're old timers, and not the freshers we were, he wants to go out.

I hide my automatic frown and make myself smile instead, even though he is behind me and can't see it.

"If you want to," I say.

"Don't just do it for me," he replies,

kissing me on the top of my head. "Only come out if *you* want to."

I want to be with him. We've spent most of the past three months together, but I'm not used to being in a relationship and I still can't get enough of him. It's unfair of me to make it seem that I only want to spend time with him because I've been single until recently. It's not that, at all. I enjoy being with him. I love being with him. Of course I'll go out tonight.

I turn to face him and let him see my smile.

"No. I want to. We'll have a good night." I pause and correct myself. "We'll have a great night."

His face breaks into a grin. "It'll give you a chance to dress up," he says.

I know it's probably only my anxiety making me feel this way, but my mind instantly takes his words as a criticism. I have no other reason to believe he meant them that way, but I look down and my clothes and frown. Plain black and floral dress. Thick tights. Flat pumps. Maybe I should wear a cardigan over this dress, soften my curves a little.

"I didn't mean –" He starts to apologise.

"I know," I say, as if I really believe my own words. "Silly. I know."

"Shall I ask the others?" he says.

I'm sure he knows as well as I do what the answer will be. I'm not alone in my dislike of the packed, sweaty bar. The chance of Zoe and Luke wanting to come with us is slim to zero, but I figure it's still polite to invite them along.

It's Saturday afternoon. Zoe has taken Luke into town for lunch and shopping, or at least she told him it was for lunch, and I know she won't be able to resist the shopping. Luke's pretty good though. He never complains, even when he comes along with the two of us. He's happy to carry our bags and wait patiently while we try on clothes that we rarely buy, or stare in shop windows at jewellery we can't afford on our student loans. I don't know if it is because I'm dating Carl now, or whether we've all settled into the status quo, but *the four of us* feels just right. It's like it was always meant to be this way.

If I text Zoe to ask her to go to the bar, the randomness of my suggestion will probably confuse her. Instead I'll wait for her to return.

When Zoe gets home, I wait for Luke to go into the kitchen, and then broach the subject as nonchalantly as I can.

"I'm going to the union with Carl tonight," I tell her. "Do you fancy coming?"

The answer must be *no*. I can't imagine that she would want to. She screws her eyes and looks at me, probably trying to work out if I've lost the plot. She knows how I feel about it, so it's no wonder she's looking at me as if I suggested we spend the evening on the Moon.

"Really?" she asks. "Are you sure? You must really like him, huh?"

I grin. She already knows that I do. It's been three months. All summer, the four of us here, happy together. Happy couples. Happy friends.

"Well I guess it's our last chance to hit fresher's week," she says, like she's trying to find a reason to say yes.

It's true. It's our last year. This is it.

I squeeze her in a tight hug. "It'll be bearable with you there," I squeak into her ear. "Thanks Zo."

She laughs. "You're going to be with Carl, you really don't need me."

"I always need you," I say before letting go. "Don't you forget that."

We get to the bar at just before nine, and it's already heaving. The main room buzzes with chatter and pounds with the heat of packed bodies. Even the open area just inside the doors, where students usually cluster around pool tables and arcade machines, is filled with standing students, drinking, talking and laughing, catching up with old friends and meeting new people.

I could have been part of this. I could have been into the social scene, down here every weekend, or even every night. I know that some of these students have been or will be if they've just started their courses. It's something I've never enjoyed though. I don't want to have to queue for hours for a drink I don't particularly want with people that I'm not really that bothered about talking to. That sounds harsh, I know. I've met some lovely people on my course, and I consider them friends, but apart from that I've spent nearly all my social time as I did before I came to uni: with Zoe.

That changed when things happened with Carl.

"Things Happened" is the best way that I can describe it. I didn't plan on having a boyfriend, but I've heard it said that the best relationships are the ones that *aren't* planned.

Zoe is talking to me, and even though she's only a foot away, I can't hear her. I lean in, squint my eyes, and tilt my ear towards her. Carl keeps walking. He has a purposeful stride, and he's making a beeline for a miraculously empty table. His hand is still in mine, but I lag behind, trying to listen to Zoe as Carl tugs at me.

"Wait," I say as loudly as I can without shouting.

He keeps walking, so I let go of his hand and stop to hear Zo.

"It's nuts in here," she says. "I never realised there were this many students."

I nod and smile, then turn back to see Carl, twenty feet off into the crowd, pushing his way through.

Zoe sees him and laughs. "You can tell he's done this before!"

Luke isn't making any kind of valiant effort to find us seats. He's standing behind Zoe, looking shell-shocked. He's more sociable than Zoe and me, but tonight, the first night of freshers' week, looks like it's too much for him. He only came because Zoe agreed, and she is only here for me. I feel responsible and a little bit guilty. She won't hold it against me though, neither of them will.

Carl's made it to the table before we start moving towards him again. I can see him talking to a couple who reached it a split second before him. He looks over in our direction, points at us, and the two students follow his direction and look over at us. I have no idea what he has told them, but the girl nods, the boy smiles, and they walk away into the crowd. I feel a little bubble of pride. Carl managed to get us seats. I flash a smile at Zoe as the three of us hurry over to join Carl at our table.

He's already sitting when we reach him.

I bend to kiss Carl, and he moves his face, leaving me smacking my lips against air.

"Not here," he says.

I smile, and expect a smile in return, but he turns to Luke and starts talking. I glance at Zoe to see if she noticed, but she's not looking. I let out a small, relieved sigh.

"Do you want to get the first round?" Carl asks, directing the question at Luke.

Luke nods. "Sure." He turns to Zoe. "I'm going to need a hand."

"Ugh, okay," she says. She dislikes the sweaty throng as much as I do, but she wouldn't let Luke struggle.

When we've told them what we want and they start to head to the bar, I give Carl a smile, sit beside him, and hold his hand beneath the table.

"How did you persuade those guys to let us have these seats?" I ask

With a straight face he says, "I told them you're pregnant." As soon as he has said it, he laughs, but I'm speechless.

"What?" he says.

"I…" I don't know what to say. My red cheeks must be telling him everything he needs to know, but he seems oblivious. I let go of his hand, instinctively bringing my arms in front of my body, resting my hands in my lap, covering my belly, even though it's already concealed beneath the table.

I know I'm not as skinny as some of the girls here, but I've always been curvy. It's not as though I've suddenly put on weight.

I want to ask whether I look fat. I want to know if people could really think I am pregnant.

He's already started talking about something else though, and I have to angle myself in closer to be able to hear him. I'm being silly. I know I must be. Carl likes me just as I am. It's funny really, when you think about it. He lied, and it wasn't the most flattering thing he could have said, but he got us the seats, and I have to be grateful for that. Being in this bar on a Saturday night and having to stand amidst the sweaty bodies the whole time would have been too much. I get to sit with my boyfriend, my best friend, and her man. I really can't complain.

Much as I don't go in for the social scene, it's going to be a rough year. I should enjoy myself while I can, because when my lectures and placements start, I'm going to be working hard and studying harder. Carl might want to carry on partying all year, but I won't have the time or the inclination.

When Zoe and Luke get back with our drinks, I don't mention what Carl said to secure the table, and by the end of the night we are laughing so much that it's all but forgotten.

Chapter Two

It's been great having time off over the summer, especially because I spent it with Carl and Zoe. And Luke of course. Carl's my boyfriend, Zoe's my best friend, but Luke is still a good mate. It's been super being with all three of them. Still, I'm excited to get back to classes, and by Monday morning I am practically buzzing to get into my lecture room.

This year's modules focus on leadership, and preparing us for making the transition from students to actual, qualified junior midwives. It still feels like an immense step, and that's because it is. The newly qualified midwives that I have met on the wards have all had preceptors to support them through their first few months after qualification, so it's not like I will be thrown in at the deep end on my own. There's always someone on hand that can reach in and pull me up if I start to flounder.

Back in the classroom on the first day of term our chatter alternates between excitement and nervousness. This is it. Our final year. We will walk out of here next

August as fully qualified midwives, ready to start our new jobs, and begin our dream careers.

Zita Somerville, one of my favourite lecturers, has judged the feeling in the room perfectly, but then again, I'm sure she's been through this before. Perhaps every group of final year students experience the same set of mixed emotions.

I'm practically prickling with apprehension. I'm surprised my anxiety hasn't kicked in, full force, but since I've been with Carl, I've been so much more relaxed and in control of my feelings. He's given me a kind of confidence I never imagined I could have. It's a good job, because I have a lot to learn this year and, as I keep reminding myself, it's going to be tough.

"In less than a year, you will be handing back your lilac tops and navy pants, leaving your student days behind you," Zita says.

She pauses to look around the room, gauging the effect of her words. As anticipated, we are all turning to our classmates, sharing the realisation that this is the final stretch.

"If you don't feel ready yet, don't worry. You're not alone. Throughout the course you've supported each other, and we have supported you. By the end of summer term, you'll be applying for jobs, and looking forward to the next steps in your careers. And you will be ready."

I gulp in air loudly and a little too sharply and let out a flurry of coughs. Everyone turns to look at me, and I feel my face start to burn as I try to calm myself.

"Same," Sophie whispers next to me. She pats me gently on the back, with a concerned look on her face.

I get in control of my breathing and manage to smile.

On the other side of her Ashley is nodding too. Zita is right: we are all in this together.

"Your Practice Assessment Documents are non-negotiable. All your competencies *must* be signed off in order for you to complete the course and qualify. When you go home today, check through your PADs. Make sure you know what you need to do and start to plan towards getting your sign-offs. You should have received your placement allocations. If you need to make any changes, speak to your link tutor as soon as possible."

I'll have placements on each of the maternity wards this year. I need little bits of everything for my PAD: I need to get more checks signed off on the postnatal and antenatal wards; I still need to assist at the births of eleven more babies. That's going to be the challenging part. Antenatal, postnatal, and infant checks are easy to come by. There are lots of women and babies on the wards, and I'm reasonably confident that getting my sign-offs won't be a problem. The deliveries are a different matter.

There's not always a labouring woman when I am on the delivery suite. When I do look after women in labour, they don't always give birth while I am on shift. Add to that the women who develop complications and need to have instrumental deliveries by forceps or ventouse, and those who have unplanned Caesareans, and my chance for getting those sign-offs reduces even further.

"If you need more time in any of the placement areas, it can be arranged. We haven't supported you this far to let you fail. You *can* do this, and you *will* do it."

Zita is saying exactly what I need to hear right now, and from the relieved murmurs that are passing around the room, I'm definitely not alone.

In the morning coffee break I have my first chance to catch up with Soph, Ashley and Simon since the summer break. Soph and Ashley have been house-sharing since last year and they're thick as thieves. I know they've probably been sharing their worries and excitement since they came back from the holidays. For Simon and me, this is our first chance to catch up face-to-face. He's the first to start off-loading.

"I'm never going to get there," he says. "I have like twenty deliveries to do."

It's not completely about the numbers. Each woman, each baby, each family, they're all important and I don't want to lose sight of that. Still, when we sit around one of the clunky plastic tables on our hard plastic chairs, the conversation quickly turns to our PADs and what we still need to get signed off to qualify.

"Ugh," Sophie groans. "I'm not even on delivery suite for the first placement."

We shake our heads in shared sympathy.

"Good to be back though," I say, trying to lighten the mood.

"It's great being back," Sophie says in agreement.

I don't see these three as much as maybe I could outside of classes, but I care about them and how they're doing. The whole class feels like it's a community; training to be a midwife is a bonding experience. It's hard to explain how it feels to be on the communal journey with these other students. We have something in common that ties us on a deeper level. We all know what the others are going through. We have similar experiences and stresses, and the same joys.

There's a buzz that comes from being present at a birth and helping a new life into the world that you can't get from anything else. Not just that, when you deliver a baby, you're helping to create a family. You're present at the most intimate, special time and that's always going to feel like a privilege. I'll never reduce that to making up the numbers I need for my portfolio.

Of course, I'm worried about getting everything signed off, but I can't let that take

over. I have to keep my anxiety under
control and focus on what matters, what
really matters.

Chapter Three

Monday afternoons have been established as my mate date time with Zoe. Even over the summer we carried on the tradition, whether we had spent the day together at home or not. This time feels special and safe; in a way it's sacred. Zoe's classes finish at lunchtime today, and mine run on until four, so I wander down from uni to the town centre on my own.

My head is full of everything I have to do in the next few months. A few months. That's all that lie between me and my future as a qualified midwife. Tick the boxes, write my research project, pass my other assessments, including that final OSCE. It's a cold October day, and I'm already cosying inside my duffle coat, but I get an extra chill thinking about that exam.

OSCE is an acronym for the Objective Structured Clinical Examination, a scenario-based practical that I have had to pass each year to continue. The first year I had a major panic attack and had to resit. Last year, I aced it. I'd love to be able to say that I am feeling calm and confident, but speaking in public isn't my strong suit, even when it's only in front of a couple of lecturers and a stand-in patient. That's not until spring; I'm not going to let myself think about it anymore just yet.

Instead, I kick through the leaves, and let my mind wander ahead of me to the coffee shop. For the first two years it was an independent café called *Blackheath's* but over the summer it's been taken over by a Coffee Express franchise. It's lost some of its unique charm, but the coffee is still good, and Zoe and I have our special corner that we aren't going to let go of in a hurry.

Sure enough, when I arrive at the door, I see her, already drinking her extra-hot-extra-shot mocha. There's another mug on the table: my latte, waiting for me.

"Thanks Zo," I say, leaning across to hug hello.

She nods. "It was my turn," she smiles. "At least I think it was."

We don't really keep count, so it doesn't matter. I settle down into my usual seat, tuck my jacket over the back of the chair, and flop my bag onto the floor.

"Busy day?" she asks.

"Aren't they all?" I say.

She tightens her lips and nods. "Seems that way. I've got so much to finish."

Even though we're studying different courses we both have assignments to write and portfolios to complete. She's going to be a teacher; I'm going to be a midwife. Everything that we have worked towards, not only at university, but before that, school, A-Levels, everything, it's finally getting us to where we always dreamed we would be.

"But we *have* nearly finished," I say.

She raises her eyebrows. "You must have had a good day," she says. "Feeling confident?"

I let out a small laugh. "Confident? I wouldn't go that far."

"You're doing great," she says. "When was the last time you had a wobble?" A wobble. I much prefer her referring to my anxiety attacks like that. It makes them sound much less intimidating. "I can't remember," she continues. "It's been so long."

"I know, me neither." I grin. I never imagined I could get to this point. "Carl makes me feel like I can do anything."

"It's not just him," Zoe smiles. "You can take some of the credit for your own achievements, you know."

I wrinkle my nose dismissively and bat the idea away.

"And stop that," she says. "It's true. You have changed such a lot."

"Changed?" I can't help but feel a stab of concern at the word, even though I'm pretty sure she doesn't mean it in bad way. It's a reflex reaction. However much I have changed, my instinct still flips back to self-doubt.

Zoe settles her coffee cup down onto the shiny white Coffee Express saucer, covering up the bean-shaped logo.

"When you started your course you were so excited, but you were so scared. Now…" She pauses, leans back on her chair, and looks at me. "Now you look like you can do anything."

"Well," I say. "It may *look* that way, but I actually feel a lot like a duck."

She tilts her head and regards me silently, waiting for an explanation.

"You know," I say. "I may look calm and

serene on the surface, but underneath my little legs are paddling like mad to keep me afloat."

Zoe bursts out into a raucous laugh that has everyone in the coffee shop turning to look at us. The barista glares over in our direction; Silvie, who worked behind the counter at Blackheath's would no doubt have come over to share the joke. Things change. Things always change.

I join in with the laughter, unable to stop myself.

Eventually, Zoe catches her breath, shakes her head, and pats my arm softly. "A duck. That's perfect."

"I waddle like one too," I say, without thinking.

Zoe rolls her eyes and tuts. "Less of that. In fact, less of that and more cake. What do you want?"

She never lets me put myself down; she's always there for me, fighting for me, and supporting me, even when I'm not supporting myself.

Chapter Four

I already have a vague idea about what I
want to focus on for my research project. It's
a subject that's close to home, but also
something that I know I have so much more
to learn about. Maternal mental health. It
was a done deal when I went to the mother
and baby unit for one of my SPOKE
placements last year. We have a module on
maternal mental health, but I am hungry to
find out more.

I haven't forgotten my visit to the Linden
Unit last spring, and I don't think I ever will.
I don't expect I'll see Meg, the mother we
visited on the unit, again, but I think of her
often. Even though I only spent a morning
with her, the experience has stayed with me.

Some of the fascination with the topic
must come from my own anxiety issues, of
course. Not only because I have been dealing
with them for so long, but also because I
wonder what it will be like for me if and
when I decide to have a child. If I'm still
going through the ups and downs of anxiety,
will I be able to cope with the stresses of
childbearing and childbirth? If I struggle at

least I will know that there is help and support available. If I struggle I will know that I'm not the only one. Maternal mental health support is so important, and I want to make sure that I always give the best I can.

I must think about exactly what it is that I want to concentrate on. The paper is six thousand words on the subject of my choosing. That's a lot of work, and there's sixty credits riding on this, so I'd better make the right decision. I want it to be interesting, but I want to write about something manageable. There are entire postgraduate courses on the topic of maternal mental health, so I have to take one fragment and focus.

When I discuss it with Sophie, Simon, and Ashley, I get the response that I had expected.

"Maternal mental health? You mean postnatal depression?" Sophie says.

"I was thinking more of antenatal issues." I watch her face change in recognition.

"Right," she says. "I hadn't thought much about that."

We don't have our mental health module until next term, and perhaps she has been fortunate enough not to encounter any women in practice with antenatal mental health support needs yet. We are only on our antenatal placements for such a narrow window of time that it's impossible to experience everything.

"I guess we'll all learn more about it after Christmas," I smile. "I've been really interested in it since I went to the Linden Unit though."

Ashley nods. "I wish I had gone somewhere like that. Might see if I can get a day booked in."

"I totally recommend it," I say.

"I'm going to write my paper on pain relief in labour," Simon says.

We all mumble affirmations at the same time. In a way I'm glad we didn't talk about my project for too long, because I don't want to end up talking about myself. That's one of the many problems with anxiety, once people know that you suffer, they want to know more, they want to try to help you, and whilst that might sound like a good thing, sometimes, most of the time, I just want to be seen as normal.

When we get back into the lecture room, our

lecturer Zita runs around the class, asking each of us to give a summary of what we are planning to write about. I think it's to give some ideas to those who haven't thought of anything yet, and surprisingly there are a handful of students that seem to have no clue. I feel lucky to have something that I am passionate about, and then as that thought strikes me I realise that I feel that way because of my own issues, just as much as my experience on the Linden Unit. It's not exactly a blessing.

The class are considering a wide range of subject areas. It's amazing how many niche areas of interest there are within pregnancy, childbirth and maternity care. There's the physiological side – one of the girls wants to explore the effects of hormones in pregnancy, the social element – another plans to write about domestic abuse, which is unfortunately a huge issue, and the emotional and mental health aspects, like my project. Then there's the practice-based issues, such as pain relief in labour or management of the third stage of labour. There's enough research on how to deliver the placenta to make it suitable as a topic for

a six-thousand-word dissertation. The more I
think about it, the more I realise how little I
know and how much I will still have to learn
once I have qualified. Being a midwife is
about being a lifelong learner; there's always
going to be something new to study and
understand.

After class, before I go to meet Zoe, I pop
into the library. The clinical side of my
training might be the most interesting and
enjoyable, but I need to remind myself to get
down to the academic work too. It's no easy
ride, training to be a midwife. It's a degree
course, and rightly so. The amount of detail
and depth that I need to include in the
written assignments leaves me with two or
three pages of references to write every time.
I'm not a naturally clever person, and it has
taken me a lot of work to get to where I am
today. I'll have to put in a lot of effort to
make sure this project is as good as it can
possibly be. I don't need to come out at the
end of the year with a first class degree, and
based on my results so far there's not much
chance of that, but I need to pass, and for the
sake of my own pride and achievement I

would like to do as well as I possibly can.

Zoe coasts through assignments and coursework. Even back at school she was so much smarter than I. Of course, Zoe being Zoe she tried to coach me and give me study skills tips, but at the end of the day I lack that certain something that she has in spades. She still offers to read my essays for me, and does the modern-day equivalent of dotting my 'i's and crossing my 't's.

Most of the books and journals are online now, but being in the library makes me feel somehow more focussed on studying. I want to take some proper ink-on-paper textbooks home with me, and the library is well-stocked with a wide array of texts on maternal mental health. This is where I will start. Get an overview, find my direction, make a plan. It sounds so easy, thinking about it like that, but I have a sneaking suspicion that these six-thousand-words are going to be terribly hard work.

Chapter Five

Before I know it, it's time to be back in my clinical placement. I get the familiar buzz of excitement as I walk through the hospital car park, past reception, up in the lift and along the corridor to the double doors. It's a route I've taken many times over the past couple of years, and if I get a job here when I qualify it will be my route to work for the foreseeable future. Even though I need to focus on getting my PAD signed off and passing my assessments, I can't help but think of the future, dangling just beyond my fingertips.

When I get onto the ward, my mentor, Jade, is already in the midwives' office, halfway through a mug of tea.

"Violet, hi!" She pulls a file off the chair next to her and pats the seat in invitation.

"Hi!" I chirp back. I know I sound overexcited, but it's because I am. I don't see the point in trying to hide it. Being enthusiastic about being here can't be a bad thing.

"Tea's fresh. Welcome home," she smiles.

Home. It does feel like that. Or at least this feels like a homecoming. I flick my gaze over to the board on the wall where all the patients' names are recorded. It's empty. My excitement sinks like a lead weight into my gut. I pour myself a tea and settle back next to Jade.

I know I have five weeks here, but I had hoped to start getting my paperwork signed off today. I don't want to start thinking in numbers instead of thinking about each woman I support, but I'd I don't get my PAD signed off I don't qualify; it's as simple as that.

"It's been a quiet week," Jade says. "I don't know what people were doing nine months ago, but they weren't making babies."

I almost snort my tea out in a heavy laugh, and manage to just about keep it in. That sets Jade off, and we are both in fits of giggles when the ward sister walks in.

"Did I miss something?" she asks.

Jade shakes her head. "You had to be there."

The ward sister shrugs and smiles. "Looks like it's going to be a quiet one," she tells us.

"Good chance to do some stock checks."

Jade nods, but my heart sinks again. I know it's something that needs to be done, but I'm here to learn. I'm here to look after women. I'm also here to get those sign-offs on my PAD.

If there aren't any patients, there's not a lot I can do.

I spend the morning checking expiry dates on the bags of fluid in the stock room and making sure the resuscitation units are fully stocked. It gives me a chance to run through some of the neonatal emergency procedures with Jade though. As we check each of the pieces of equipment and drugs on the trolley, she asks me questions, and I quick-fire the answers confidently.

There's an hour and a half left of my shift when the phone finally rings.

"Delivery suite. Student midwife speaking." I say, as cheerfully as I can.

"Hi Delivery Suite Student Midwife, it's Antenatal Ward Student Midwife."

I recognise Sophie's voice immediately.

"Hi Soph. What's up?"

"I've got a lady for you. She's been here

since the early hours. Debbie Baker, primp, term plus one. She was having contractions and wasn't sure if she had ruptured membranes or not."

Ruptured membranes sounds terribly dramatic, but it's only a technical term for the waters breaking.

"She's contracting now, every four minutes, and she wants some analgesia. I've done a VE and she's five centimetres."

VE is shorthand for vaginal examination. The cervix opens up to ten centimetres at full dilatation. In first-time mums it can feel a little bit like a firm long nose with a tiny dimple to start with. It gets thinner and more stretchy as labour continues, until you can't feel any of it at all. The wonders of the human body will never be lost on me.

Five centimetres might sound like it's halfway through labour, but that's not always the case. It's not steady progress, although a rough guide is that cervices dilate at around a centimetre per hour. Women are unpredictable and cervices even more so.

Even at full dilatation, the baby needs to descend down the birth canal before its mother is able to push it out. I would say that birth takes time and it's a long slow process, but there are also those women who sprint from onset of labour to delivery in minutes rather than hours. I hope that if I ever have a baby I'm one of the quick ones.

"Okay," I say. "Thanks Sophie. Nothing else I need to know?"

"Routine pregnancy. No medical history. Her partner is coming up with her."

"Great. Are you bringing her? I'll get a room ready."

"Yes, I'll bring her up. See you soon."

It's not likely that Debbie will give birth while I'm still on shift, but I love the whole process. Supporting women and their partners through labour is one of my favourite parts of midwifery.

Sophie, Debbie, and a man that Soph introduces as Marcus, Debbie's partner, arrive on the ward within five minutes.

I run through the usual orientation to the ward, showing Debbie where the toilet and the call button are, and I get handover from Soph while Debbie settles in.

"No one about?" Sophie says, casting her gaze over the empty board on the office wall.

"Really quiet," I say. "We've been

checking resuscitaires and doing a stock count."

Soph pulls her face without thinking. "Not going to get any deliveries like that," she says. "I need ten more."

"I need eleven," I tell her, and she pulls her face again.

"I know," I say, trying to smile. "Busy downstairs?"

She wobbles her hand in a so-so movement. "Quiet everywhere, I think."

"Typical. I bet they were rushed off their feet until we started our placements."

The university try to arrange our placements so there aren't too many students on any ward at the same time, but there are weeks when we are all in our lecture blocks, and we all have annual leave at Christmas, Easter and summer break. It would be just my luck if every woman in town had already delivered while I was in university.

Sophie pats my hand. "We'll get there," she smiles.

"We will," I say. I know we have to.

When I go back into her room, Debbie is standing by the side of the bed, sucking on the gas and air like it's her life support system. As her contraction subsides I rest my hand on her arm and encourage her to let go of the tubing that's delivering her pain relief.

"Take some breaths. Get some fresh air in between contractions," I say

"I feel woozy," she says, with an unsteady wobble in her voice that confirms it.

"Hop up. Take a seat on the bed for a minute." I guide her, supporting her as she moves.

The gas and air can do that to some women. Just enough of it takes the edge off the contractions, too much and it can cause a fuzzy dizziness.

Debbie hauls herself awkwardly onto the bed and sits, eyes closed, head pressed back against the two pillows.

Bedding is sparse in the delivery room. There are two sheets on the bed: one that covers the whole mattress and then another that lies horizontally across it, lined with a plastic underlay. It's positioned directly beneath Debbie's bottom, as intended. There's also a large square incontinence pad, the same kind that the nurses use on the wards, but for our patients it's more frequently used for catching vaginal fluids rather than urine. There's usually some discharge during labour, and a little blood loss can be normal too. The other fluid we look for is the water from the amniotic sac. Soph said they haven't had any confirmation that the waters have broken, and as yet I haven't seen anything either.

I carry out a full set of observations as a baseline, check Debbie's blood pressure, temperature and pulse, listen to baby's heartbeat, and make a note of how regular the contractions are, how strong, and how long they last. Everything is recorded on something we call a MEOWS chart, which gives an at-a-glance view of how things are advancing, changing, or not changing throughout labour.

MEOWS is another of those acronyms that makes maternity-speech sound like a different language. I've picked most things up so far, but every now and again I hear something new and have to ask for an explanation. Saying "MEOWS" is a lot easier than constantly referring to the Modified Early Obstetric Warning Score, that's for sure.

Everything seems absolutely fine.

I sit with Debbie and Marcus, chatting, observing, and recording the regular, routine checks. Without warning, during one particularly gripping contraction, Debbie grunts loudly.

"I need to push," she says. "I really need to push."

I look over to Jade. This is quicker than we would expect in a first-time mum, but as I've said, women's bodies are unpredictable.

"All through your contraction or just when it's at its peak?" I ask.

"At its peak, I think. When it's really strong."

"Okay," I say. "Let me know when you get your next one. Tell me what it feels like." Then I add, "Have you been to the toilet recently?"

"She went about half an hour ago," Marcus says.

"I tried," she says. "I couldn't do anything."

"Baby's head is right down there between the bowels and the bladder. It might just be that you can feel," I say.

As I'm finishing the sentence, Debbie

clenches her hands into fists, grabbing the sheet. Marcus holds the mouthpiece up to Debbie's face, and supports her as she takes big deep breaths of the gas and air.

She breathes steadily at first. In and out. Deep and slow. Then, as the contraction builds, her eyes widen, and she lets out another grunt.

"I need to push now," she growls from behind the mouthpiece.

"See if you can see anything," Jade says from behind me.

"Okay Debbie. If you don't mind, I'm going to take a look down below and see if there's any signs that baby might be coming."

She nods her consent. "That's fine," she breathes.

I raise the sheet and look at Debbie's vulva for any signs of movement, or for any signs of an approaching baby. There's nothing yet. I place my hand onto her uterus, feeling the contraction. It's strong and firm, but it doesn't feel like she's pushing.

There's a difference in the feel of an expulsive contraction that's pushing a baby out and the regular labour contractions. If she's feeling the urge, she's not acting on it yet. If she can hold it back then maybe it's not time yet.

"I can't stop," she says. "I really need to push."

"Keep breathing, Debbie. Use the gas and air." Jade says.

When the contraction settles off, Jade speaks to me. "See if you can get her to the loo, and if she's still feeling the urge you'd better examine her and find out what's going on."

I nod and turn back to Debbie to get her consent.

After a slow hobble to the toilet and back, I start the examination. She's still only five centimetres. No change. She's definitely not ready to push yet.

"Can I push?" she growls as her next contraction starts to peak.

"Not yet," I say. She closes her eyes and breathes deeply, and I turn to Jade and hold up five fingers.

"It's not time yet," Jade says. "You're still five centimetres. It's going to be a little while longer."

"No!" Debbie shouts, opening her eyes

wide. "I can't do it. I can't. It's too much."

She looks over at her husband, and he rushes to stand back by her side.

"Easy," he says. "You can do it. You can."

"I want an epidural. I want one now," she says.

"That might be a good idea," Jade says. "If you're getting that urge to push already, we really need you to not push. If you push and you're not ready, you can make your cervix swell up, and it will make things take even longer."

"She *doesn't* want an epidural," her husband says. "She was going to write a birth plan. We never got round to it, but she said that she definitely doesn't want an epidural."

"I. Want. An. Epidural," Debbie repeats. "I don't care what I said before; I want one now."

I nod, and Jade gives Marcus a little shrug.

"Sometimes we don't know what we want until we are in labour. No one can imagine what it is going to be like until they are here." Jade turns to Debbie. "It means that

42

you will need to stay on the bed and be monitored throughout your labour. We will keep a track of baby's heartbeat on the CTG monitor here, and Violet will be checking your blood pressure and pulse."

"It's not long since you were last examined, so I'm not worried about the cervix not having changed much yet," Jade says. "But if it does look like things are moving slowly we can give you something to speed things up a bit. If we do that, you'll be glad of the epidural."

"Okay," she says. "Get it now, please."

Marcus speaks gently to his wife. "Are you sure this is what you want?"

The look she gives him is resolute, but I'm sure I see a tinge of sadness.

"I'm sorry," Debbie says. "I need the epidural. I wanted to manage without, but I can't. I'm sorry."

"Don't be sorry, love. If you need it, you need it. I'm right here."

Jade and I smile at each other before she heads into the corridor to page the anaesthetist. With an hour left of my shift it's unlikely I'll be present at the delivery, but I know that I am learning with every woman I care for, and with every situation I deal with. I wish I could stay with Debbie, but by the time the anaesthetist has arrived, set up and given her the epidural it's time for me to leave.

Debbie looks calm and comfortable, and I know that I have done everything that I could to support her this afternoon. This is the way that it will be throughout my midwifery career. I will deliver many babies, but I will care for women through pregnancy, labour and beyond without having the honour of being present for the births. If Debbie is still in the postnatal ward tomorrow afternoon I'll go up and visit her, but this is where my journey with her ends, at least for this pregnancy.

"Good luck," I say, as I finish handing over to the afternoon staff.

There's a first-year student, a shy-looking girl called Priti, who will be taking over where I have left off. I hope she gets to be present at the birth.

"And good luck to you," I whisper to her, as I pass by and make my way to the locker room.

Chapter Six

Despite the quiet, slow start, by the end of my first week back on placement, I have added three more deliveries to the signed sheet in my PAD. I'm constantly aware that we are halfway through November, and time is ticking away. I need to start my assignment and finalise my project plan. I'm starting to feel overwhelmed by the amount of work I have to do and pressured by the boxes I have to tick to complete my PAD. When weekend arrives all I want to do is spend time with Carl.

Even though we have been dating for four months now, I still sleep alone, in my own room. It was my decision, not his. If we had met some other way there's no way that we would be living together or spending every night together this early in a relationship. I'm starting to understand some of the things that Zoe must have experienced with Luke last year. He was a housemate, and then a friend, and then her lover; I didn't realise how complicated that could be. Exciting, but complicated.

Nine thirty, Saturday morning, there's a light tapping on my door. I've been awake for a while, but I'm still in bed, lazily flicking through the pages of a sweet romantic novel that Zoe passed on to me. It's building up to a crucial scene, but as soon as I hear the knocking, I slide in my bookmark, straighten my hair with my fingers and call out, "Hello?"

"Breakfast, Princess."

Carl nudges the door open with a firm buttock, and edges into my room carrying a wooden tray. On it he has laid out cereal, coffee, toast, and orange juice. He sets the tray on my desk. I give him a big grin and shuffle my legs over to the side so that he can perch on the edge of my bed.

"Hey," I say. "Thank you. You didn't need to…"

Before I can finish my appreciative gushing, he silences me with a kiss.

"You've had a busy week," he says. "Anything for you."

This is way better than the romance in my book. This is real. This is what people do when they love one another. And he does. I do. We're in love. This is perfect.

"It *has* been crazy," I say with a smile. "I'm sorry that we haven't seen each other much."

He shakes his head. "Don't worry about it. I knew what I was getting into. I've been fine here on my own with the lovebirds, watching the same old shows."

I laugh, and he smiles.

"Didn't you go out last night?" I ask. "I knocked on your door when I came home and…"

He kisses me again, and the peck turns into a long, deep embrace. I melt into him and wish that every day were a day off for me. I wish I could be with Carl all the time, but that's not how things are. Most weekends I'll be lucky to have even one day with him, so I should be thrilled to have both Saturday and Sunday at home this week. Zoe suggested a trip to the shops, but I know she understood when I said I'd like to see Carl. Anyway, it will make my regular Monday mate date with Zoe all the better if we wait another couple of days to catch up.

"Hey. Anyone home?" Carl waves his hand in front of my eyes and I realise that I was floating away with my thoughts of coffee, cake and chatting to my best mate.

"Sorry!"

I smile and lean back into him, hoping to repeat the hug we just enjoyed. Instead, he pats me gently and moves to stand up.

"Get your breakfast in you. We're going out today."

"Oh?" I say. "We are? Where to?"

"That, my sweet Violet, is a surprise."

A judder of excitement passes through me.

"I love surprises!" I say.

"I hope you'll love this one," he says, "but don't get *too* excited."

How can I not?

I practically bolt my breakfast, or at least I eat it as quickly as I can without looking too much of a glutton. I don't want Carl thinking I'm a complete pig. He's got the toast spot-on, exactly as I like it. He must have been paying attention, all the times that I've made breakfast over the past few months. The thought makes a little warm glow bloom in my chest. It's such a good feeling to know that there's someone as lovely as Carl that actually *loves* me.

Carl doesn't have a car. I guess there's no

point when all we do is walk to uni or walk into town. I'm sure he had one when he first moved in last year, but I wasn't paying nearly enough attention to him then, and it doesn't seem all that important now. Either way, Carl's lack of a car means that he leads me to the bus stop, and then on to the train station, where we catch the 11:42 in the direction of London.

It's the end of November, but as we snuggle together in the train seats, sharing his set of earphones I feel cosy and warm. I still don't know where we are going, but the choice of train has narrowed it down to somewhere in the New Forest (squee! Pony rides! A spa day? No, because he didn't tell me to bring anything. Lunch in a country pub?) Southampton (yes! Shopping and food!) or London (could be anything, but everything I can think of is exciting). Lots of people might have been pestering their boyfriend to tell them where they are going, but I've settled into the thrill of the surprise.

We chat about everything and nothing as the train takes us through the Forest and on towards the suburbs of Southampton City. When we pull into Southampton station, Carl moves to stand up without saying anything, and I scrabble hurriedly to my feet. I haven't finished my three pounds train tea, and I would usually hate to leave it behind, but today I don't care. Today I hold onto my boyfriend's hand, my cheeks glow with the excitement rather than the cold, and I follow.

Along the high street, in front of the tall department stores and glass-fronted clothes shops, wooden huts bustle with throngs of shoppers. There's a heavy scent of cinnamon and sweetness in the air, and my mouth is practically watering as we push through the crowds. Still with his hand in mine, Carl leads me past cabin after cabin, pausing with me as I stop to point at whatever catches my eye.

"These hats!" I squeal, picking up a knitted headpiece with two long flaps, designed to look like spaniel ears.

Carl smiles, and patiently lets me put the hat onto his head. It suits him. Even something this silly can't make him look anything other than perfect. The fact that he is happy for me to put it on him in the first place makes him even more perfect, in my eyes.

"Am I your little puppy dog?" he laughs, trying to give me a puppy-dog-eyed look.

All I can do is laugh back. It's an icy cold day, but I can barely feel it.

Being with him is so easy.

I'm still full from the breakfast he made me when we reach the bratwurst stand.

"Sausage?" Carl asks.

"I…"

Before I can say no, he's ordering an extra large with onions and cheese.

"Same for you?" he says.

"I don't know if –"

Again, he doesn't wait for a reply. I can probably manage it. His is already on the counter, and it smells amazing. He squirts on the ketchup and mustard and leaves me to collect my hotdog as he pays.

"Do you want to get some drinks?" I ask.

He's got a mouthful of food, so he shakes his head and raises a hand.

After he's gulped it down he says, "Let's wait and get a mulled wine or hot chocolate."

He takes another bite and nods in the direction of the large building in the middle of the square. It's a mock Alpine lodge, complete with bar and kitsch cable cars that customers can sit in while they drink. Much as I'm enjoying my bratwurst now that I have it, I can't wait to get a hot chocolate.

"Okay," I grin.

There was a time that I would avoid coming out into crowded places like this. My anxiety would start to rise as soon as I sensed the people all around me, and I couldn't relax until I got into some space. Now I feel a serene, strange calmness, and dare I say happiness, sitting here while shoppers hurry past us. It's almost as though I am enclosed in a bubble. It's like being in one of those cable cars, high above the snowy hills, but safe from the ground below and protected from the cold.

I finish my food and wipe a smudge of mustard off my jacket sleeve stealthily, so that Carl doesn't notice what a clumsy oaf I am.

Of course, he sees, and he flashes a grin.

"We can buy some for the house, you know. You don't need to smuggle it home on your clothing."

"Just trying to save us some money." I go

along with it. "My student loan is already out of control."

He smiles and pats my arm gently, as if in sympathy rather than jokingly. I guess it wasn't all that funny.

"Listen," he says. "Save these seats and I'll go and get the drinks."

"Sure," I shrug.

It *is* busy, and if we both get up and go to the bar we will probably have nowhere to sit when we come back.

He doesn't ask what I want and sets off towards the lodge.

I sit and watch the couples walking arm in arm, the parents being pulled along by their children from stall to stall. My eye is drawn to a pregnant woman looking at hand-knitted jumpers. Even when I'm not on my placements I'm curious about expectant mothers. She looks about eight months pregnant, and as I watch her holding the knitwear up to herself I wonder what it would be like to have a Christmas baby.

She must be booked to deliver in Southampton, I'll probably never see her again, but I still start to daydream about how her birth will go. I feel a kinship with pregnant women. We are part of the same team, even when I'm not in my uniform.

Carl nudges my arm. "Hey," he says.

He puts a purple mug down on the table in front of me. Hot chocolate, with a thick swirl of cream and chocolate sprinkles. Just what I would have ordered. Actually, I would probably have skipped the cream and sprinkles, even though I want them. I don't want to stuff myself in front of Carl. I mean logically I know that he doesn't care what I eat. I know he loves me (yay!) just the way I am, but a part of me is still hopelessly self-conscious. I remember my dad scrutinising my food and drink choices when I was budding from a child to an adolescent. I'm used to feeling bad about my decisions.

"Hey," Carl says again.

"Thanks!" I grin, blushing. "That looks perfect!"

"Not as perfect as you." He bends and kisses me before taking his seat next to me.

It doesn't feel sickly sweet, it feels right, and I accept the compliment just as readily as the hot chocolate.

"Thinking about your course?" he asks, following my line of vision to the lady I was watching.

"Always," I say. "I mean, not always. That's not what I meant. I mean…"

He smiles and hugs me into him. "I know what you mean, silly."

Will I ever get used to not worrying about saying the wrong thing? I hope so.

When Carl sits down there's a moment of silence between us, and it feels like there's something heavy in the air. For some reason I can sense he is going to say something important. It's like when a storm is brewing, and you haven't felt the rain or heard thunder, but the air is pregnant with the coming change.

I keep quiet and look at him expectantly.

He shifts a little in his seat and takes a drink from his mulled wine, not looking me in the eye. He looks around casually and then clears his throat before speaking.

"I told my parents I'll be bringing you home for Christmas," Carl says. His face is beaming. "I can't wait for you to meet them."

We spent most of the summer break at Tangiers Court together. I assumed that I'd be going to see my mum at Christmas. I haven't made actual plans, but mentally I was sure that was what would happen. Mum will be on her own if I don't go home. I can't leave her alone over Christmas. I'm too stunned to speak. I don't know what to say.

"I'll take you to meet my friends too. There's loads of places I want to go with you."

He gives me a squeeze that feels too tight. He's warm and close and I need some air. I need to think. I need to breathe.

"Okay," I say, without meaning it as an acceptance. "I mean that's a nice idea. I…I don't know. I don't know if I can. I want to. I do. But…"

He doesn't say anything as I stutter my words, feeling hotter and hotter.

I should have thought about this. I should have brought it up earlier, let him know how I felt before he started to make plans. I've messed everything up.

"My mum has booked a restaurant for dinner Christmas Day," he says flatly. "We make a big deal of it. It's a family tradition."

I don't want an argument; all I want is time to think.

He's gone from looking full of happiness to having an expression of almost anger. I can understand him being disappointed by my response, but it feels like more than that.

"I'll…" I'm trying to think and speak at the same time, and it's not working very well. "I'll have to talk to Mum." It's the best I can manage.

"Okay," he says in a voice that makes me think that it's very much not okay.

I have to say more. I have to give more than this.

"I want to be with you," I say. "I want to spend Christmas with you so much." I do. It's not in any way a lie.

"That's great," he smiles. "I'll tell Mum we are definitely going."

I want to say, '*wait, no,*' but instead I gulp, pick up my mug and drink. It tasted so perfectly sweet before, but now it's somehow sickly.

I don't know how I'm going to explain this to Mum. She barely saw me all summer, and now I'm not even going to spend the festive holidays with her. I sigh softly as the thoughts swim around my head.

Carl is oblivious; he smiles and gently

brushes a loose hair from my cheek.

"It's going to be perfect," he says. "Just like my perfect Violet."

Chapter Seven

The rest of the day feels overcast, the cloud of our conversation hovering above us. It should be a wonderful day, but I have ruined it by not being confident enough to speak my mind. Instead I have contained the worry inside of me, and I can feel it simmering.

When we get back to Tangiers Court, late afternoon, I want to talk to Zoe about everything straight away. Living with Carl means there's not much opportunity for a private conversation. We enter the house together, sit in the living room together, and there's no chance of me slipping out to talk to Zoe without drawing attention.

Perhaps my worry about talking to her is all in my head. After all I talk to Zoe every day; it's completely normal. Knowing that I want to tell her about my concerns makes me feel like I am going behind Carl's back, like I'm doing something wrong. Still, Zoe knows me, and she knows something is off. Even though when I talk to her I'm gushing about the woollen mittens and sickly-sweet fudge, beaming with the glow of the day with my boyfriend, she can still see the burden underneath my smiles.

When I head to the kitchen to make drinks, she pulls herself up to follow.

"You okay?" She leans against the counter while I fill the kettle.

"Yeah," I reply, not making eye contact.

"You don't seem one hundred per cent," she says. "Not coming down with something, are you?"

"No, really. I'm fine."

"Okay," she says, but she doesn't sound convinced.

Once I've added a spoonful of coffee granules into each mug there's not much else I can do other than to turn and face her.

I know that she can see it in my face, or perhaps it's in the way I hold myself, the tone of my voice, I don't know. It's instinctive, the way we pick up on each other's moods.

"Carl's invited me to his parents' for Christmas." I come out with it, just like that. There's no other way of saying it.

"Oh that's…lovely," she says. The pause between her words says more than the words themselves.

"I know. I can't leave Mum alone, can I?

It is lovely. Of course I want to be with him, but…" I let my sentence trail off and I shrug.

"Did you say no? What did you say?"

"I said I'd have to talk to Mum, but somehow, I don't know how, it seems like I've agreed to go with him. And now I can't go back on that; I have to find a way to tell Mum that I'm not going to be there. This should be a good thing, you know, having Christmas with my lovely boyfriend, meeting his family, everything."

I've not felt like this for months, not since before Carl and I were together, but now I can feel my pulse quicken and my breathing become unstable. I know I'm on the edge of an anxiety attack, and Zoe can see it too.

"Okay," she says. "It's okay. It's going to be okay."

She puts her hand onto my arm and gently guides me to one of our dining chairs.

"Sit. Come on."

Her voice is steady and calm, and I try to focus on it as she speaks softly.

"Don't worry about it. Not now. We will make it right. Okay?" She's looking at me for a reply, but my mouth is desert dry and my tongue flaps, wordless.

"I'll make the drinks. Just sit here, get some air."

She kicks the back door open and a blast of cold November air rushes in. I feel it thrill over my face, and the cooling sensation works its way into my hot skin.

My heart is pounding, but I take deep, slow breaths, trying to keep as steady as Zoe's voice.

A panic attack.

In my own home.

My safe place.

Zoe has her hand on my shoulder, grounding me. I don't know how I've got myself into this situation. Really, I should be able to talk to Carl, tell him how I feel and explain that I can't leave Mum alone. I should be able to, but if even thinking about it makes me feel like this, how am I going to be able to have a discussion with him? I thought that being with him had somehow raised my confidence, washed away some of my self-doubt and personal fears, seeing as I haven't felt the slightest trace of anxiety since I've been with him. Now that's all up in the air. I don't know anything anymore.

"What do you want to do?" She says it

with the emphasis on the word *you*.

I look over towards the door. I'm sure Carl is happily watching television with Luke, caught up in whatever is happening on *Dating Nightmares*, but still, it's possible that he could hear what we are saying. I don't want that. I don't want a confrontation or an argument. Isn't that what had got me into this situation in the first place? Not wanting an argument means that I haven't opened my mouth and spoken my mind. It feels like there's no easy solution.

"I don't want to upset anyone." I look up to Zoe, and the concern in her eyes makes me feel even worse.

"Zoe I'm sorry."

"Don't be sorry. Don't feel bad about having feelings, or about wanting to make people happy." Her voice is both soft and stern. "You've done nothing wrong."

"It doesn't feel that way."

I'm so on edge that I can tell straight away when the volume on the television lowers a couple of notches.

There's a shout from the living room.

"Did you get lost on the way?" Carl hollers.

I flash a look to Zoe and then call back, my voice as stable as I can manage. "Sorry! Nearly done!"

He knows I'm in here with Zoe. Surely he can work out that we are talking.

"Stop apologising," Zoe says. "Do you want to sit outside for a few minutes?"

I shake my head briskly. "I should take Carl his drink."

Zoe gives me a wide-eyed stare that almost looks like disappointment.

Whatever I decide to do, I'm not doing any decision making right now. Not like this.

"Give yourself some space, okay?" Zoe says, making it sound like a request when really it's a command. "You've been doing so well. You can keep on top of this."

She's so convinced, I have to nod. My heart is still heavy but it's slowing, settling back to a normal rhythm. Knowing I need to get back in to Carl isn't helping but the chill air and Zoe's chill attitude definitely are.

"Vi?" Carl calls again.

"Don't think about it now. We can have a chat about it on Monday," Zoe says. "Okay?"

I nod and get to my feet. I'm steady. I'm

in control.

I pick up Carl's mug, take it through to the living room, and settle down next to him. He reaches his arm around me and draws me in close. I breathe in his warmth and nuzzle my nose against his chest to fill my lungs with the scent of him.

Everything will be fine. I'm sure it will.

Chapter Eight

The thing about being a student midwife is that you always have to be mentally present. No matter what's going on in your personal life you have to have your head firmly on your shoulders and your focus fixed on the here and now. Today that feels like a good thing. I want to be able to think about something other than my internal debate over what I should do. Someone more decisive or self-confident might just have been able to speak their mind, but however much I have learned over the past couple of years, I'm not at that point yet.

I've been hushed down and shut up so many times, and I've stopped myself from making my opinions heard when there's even the slightest chance that they might upset someone else. I'm a people pleaser; that's what I do; that's what growing up displeasing my father taught me to do.

I snap myself back to the room and prepare to take handover. I have to leave everything else at the door, off the ward, and out of my head. Today I am on delivery suite. I am Student Midwife Violet Cobham.

I am here to support women, and hopefully deliver babies.

There's a lady due up to the ward for induction and I'm the only student on shift today. That means that unless any labouring women arrive before she comes up, I'll be responsible for looking after her. With my mentor of course. I know that I'm going to be kept occupied for the rest of the shift, but I have time to chat to my mentor before our patient arrives.

"How's the coursework going?" Jade, asks.

I sip my tea and shrug. "I'm on top of it," I say. "I'm more worried about getting my practicals signed off."

"No one has ever not managed it, Vi. Don't worry too much."

It's good to hear those words, even though the empty spaces in my PAD shout out at me every time I open my folder.

"What are you writing for your final year project?"

University sometimes feels like a different world to the placement units. Of course I am putting into practice what I learn in the classroom, and I take back to my lectures the things that I experience on placement. Trying to bundle it all together and make sense of everything, especially where there appears to be a placement-classroom divide, is a challenge.

"Um, something to do with maternal mental health," I say. My voice wavers uncertainly.

"There's lots of research on that. You should find plenty to write about."

"Too much," I agree. "I don't want to just focus on postnatal depression though."

"Interesting," Jade says. "What do you want to focus on?"

I pause for a moment before answering, trying to get my thoughts together.

"I want to write something about mental health in pregnancy," I say. "Anxiety." I leave the word dangling, wondering whether to say more. Looking over at Jade, who has supported me on my placements here since the start of the course, I decide to open up. "I have suffered myself, with anxiety I mean, for, gosh, for nearly ten years now I guess." The thought that it has been so long hits me like a sledgehammer.

"I wouldn't have known," she says. "You

always seem very confident and competent."

"I feel it," I say. "At least when I'm here I do."

"And when you're not?"

I look away, drink some more of the hot, milky tea, and pause again.

"Mostly I'm okay. Mostly."

"There's always someone here to talk to. If you need to."

Before I reply, she adds, "And I'm always here too."

"Thanks," I say.

Even though I passed up the chance to talk to a specialist last year, knowing that Jade is here for me if I do need to talk feels like a cosy relief. She knows me just enough for me to trust her, but not intimately enough for me to feel awkward talking to her. On top of that, being able to talk and listen are two of the most important skills of a midwife. She may not be a trained counsellor, but I know she has the supportive experience.

"Really," she says. "I mean it."

"Thanks, Jade."

A thought flashes through my head that maybe I could tell her what I'm feeling today, talk to her about what's on my mind, but as soon as the thought forms, I push it away. It seems silly to be worrying about something that could easily be solved by talking to my boyfriend. When I think about it that way I want to give myself a shake and have a firm word with myself.

"You've already been very helpful," I smile.

"Well, that's good," she says. "That's what I'm here for."

"That and helping me get this PAD signed off," I grin.

She smiles and shakes her head. "Really, you'll get there!"

I just about have time to drain the rest of my tea before the antenatal ward midwife brings our lady up to delivery suite. She's a first -time mum, and sometimes induction can take longer than the eight hours that I have for my shift, but you never know.

I share a positive grin with Jade and make my way to introduce myself to our patient Dina. Whether I get to deliver a baby today or not, I get to spend time with Dina and support her through one of the most special experiences of her life. After talking to Jade I'm ready to focus completely on her and on providing the best care and support I can. Everything else can wait. Today, I am here. Today I am Student Midwife Violet Cobham, and she is confident and competent.

By the time my shift is over, and I am on the bus into town to meet Zoe, thoughts of Carl are far from my mind. Being on shift has such a positive effect on me; I hope it is always this way, but there's a niggle at the back of my mind that warns me that there are going to be bad days on the ward. I'm not always going to have the energy and enthusiasm of a fresh student. I hope that whatever happens it never starts to feel like work.

"You seem happier," Zoe notices as I join her at our regular table.

I haven't actually thought any more about what I am going to say to Carl, or how I am going to approach him, but she's right. I do feel happier.

"Good day on the ward," I smile.

"Oh?" she asks. "Something exciting happen?"

Did it? Not really. Nothing out of the

ordinary. I spent time with Dina, we talked about television programmes and Christmas shopping and how much we both love this time of the year. I checked her vitals, listened to her baby, and together we waited for her contractions to begin. It was routine and unremarkable, but somehow it was still a good day.

I make a casual dismissive hum sound and shake my head.

"Well, it's nice to see you more relaxed anyway," she says.

Not that I have an agenda for the conversations with Zoe, but I had expected that we would spend the whole of our mate date talking about Carl and what I should say to him. Now that I am here, all I want to do is drink latte, laugh with my friend, and carry on feeling the light contentment that being on the ward has given me. I don't want to spend my precious time with my friend moaning about my boyfriend doing something that he obviously hasn't done to intentionally confuse or confound me.

Sometimes I snap into panic mode so quickly that I don't stop to think about what I could or should do. My instinctive response

is always to clam up, shut down and agree
with whatever other people want. When I
have time to think everything seems clearer.
I know already that all I need to do is talk to
him and explain how I feel. It's as simple as
that.

Chapter Nine

When we get back to the house, Zoe and Luke head up to her room, leaving Carl and I alone in the living room. I want to talk to him as soon as I can, so that the situation doesn't drag on, and I don't spend any longer than I need to overthinking what I am going to say. Talk to him. Explain how I feel. Simple.

We are both sitting on the sofa, angled in towards each other, relaxed and comfortable.

"Carl," I say. I already feel too formal, as soon as I say his name. I soften my voice and continue, "I would love to spend Christmas with you, and I can't wait to meet your family –"

He doesn't let me finish the sentence.

"I can tell there is a *but* coming up," he says, moving away from me ever so slightly.

My agenda must be obvious. I feel my cheeks burn and I feel a shimmer of nausea. I want to tuck my head away and hide from this conversation. I slowly make eye contact, expecting to see anger, but instead, he looks calm.

I take a breath and continue, starting with

a gentle smile.

"There is. I'm sorry."

"But?" he says.

"But I can't. I really am sorry."

"You've said you're sorry. I believe you."
He strokes my cheek, and I know he must be
able to feel the heat of my blush.

"I…my mum. I can't. I just can't leave
her on her own."

He nods slowly with a look of
disappointed understanding.

"I'm so sorry," I say. The apology keeps
falling from my lips.

"Violet!" he says. "Stop now. It's fine."

I worried since Saturday for nothing.
Instead of being embarrassed about telling
him that I couldn't go home with him after
all, I'm embarrassed that I was stupid
enough to think that Carl would be angry.

"Are you sure? I feel so bad. You made
plans and you've told your parents, and
everything you described, it all sounded so
perfect."

He shrugs. "Your mum is more important
than our perfect Christmas," he says.

My eyes flicker slightly, as I try to search
his words for meaning. I'm still not

confident enough to believe that he really is okay with what I have said.

Either way, the image of he and I in front of the log fire in his parents' house, surrounded by warmth and bustle and love starts to fade from my mind. I have to let it go. I'm making the right decision. I'm doing the right thing.

"Maybe we can have a little celebration, just the two of us, before you go home?" I suggest.

He leans back, even further away from me, and stretches his arms above his head.

"What do you think?" I persist.

"I don't know, Violet. Christmas is a special time. It wouldn't be the same, would it?"

I have to look away again as I try to gulp down the ball that's formed in my throat.

I shake my head almost imperceptibly.

"Would it?" he says again.

"No," I say. My voice is mouselike.

I force myself to lift my eyes.

"There'll be other Christmases," I say. The sound is still tiny and weak.

He's not even looking at me. Instead, he's turned his attention to the television, pressing the switch to turn it on and start scrolling through the channels.

"Carl?" I almost whisper.

"I said it's fine. Leave it." His words come out like a snarl, and he visibly stops himself before continuing to speak in a softer, more measured tone. "What would you like to watch?"

I open my mouth slightly to almost speak, but I don't think that carrying on with this conversation is going to make for a pleasant evening. Instead I force myself to smile.

"Whatever you fancy," I say. "It's nice just being here with you."

He puts his arm firmly around my shoulder and pulls me back toward him with a smooth tug that makes me slide over the sofa into his embrace. I can feel the pounding of my heart pressed into his side. He is firm and immobile next to me, more like a statue than a human.

He kisses the top of my head, his breath warm through my hair. I want to smile and snuggle against him, but I know that I have disappointed him. I've let him down, and I can't relax knowing that I have made him unhappy.

"Carl, I…"

"Ssh," he says, and presses a finger against my lips. "Don't."

And so I don't. Instead of speaking, I sit silently beside him as he watches television, and I try to think of a way to make this up to him. I have to do what's right for my mum, but I should also try to do right by Carl. If I can make him happy too, I might be able to stop the nauseating anxiety that is taking me over.

Chapter Ten

There are only two weeks left of term, two weeks to get as many deliveries signed off as I can on my placement and two weeks to feel rubbish about spending Christmas without Carl. Zoe and Luke are going to be in Portland with *her* parents this year. It's a relief to know that she will only be a short walk away from where I'm staying. Home. Didn't I used to call it home? So much has changed, but I miss my mum. I love my mum. That's never going to change.

Being on placement is a welcome distraction. It's a busy morning and Jade and I have been allocated two women today. It doesn't happen often, the ideal is that each midwife only has one woman to care for, but neither of the ladies is in active labour.

"Cherry Brady, room three. First baby; due tomorrow. Been on the antenatal ward with some protein in her urine and mild raised blood pressure. We're keeping an eye on her at the moment. Doctor Barthes is coming after his antenatal round to review. Paula Carter, room six. Thirty-nine weeks. She's had a couple of rapid deliveries in the past, came in about an hour ago with niggles. Just a multip's os, and her contractions have tailed off a bit since she arrived. I'm reluctant to let her go just yet, and Sister agreed we should keep her a couple of hours and await events. I'd have offered her a bed downstairs but they're full too."

It's a difficult call sometimes, trying to find the balance between taking up a room and providing the reassurance and care that's needed. On paper Paula could possibly go home and come back later but having already experienced two precipitate deliveries I can understand her not wanting to take the risk. I know I wouldn't want to.

There are four midwives and I on the shift and seven patients. The maths says we have to do what we can to share the workload. Not every woman can have constant one-to-one care, no matter how much I would love that to be the case. One of the skills I need to develop for my career as a midwife is knowing how to manage my workload and still give the best care and support possible to the women and families I'm responsible for.

Paula is sitting on the bed chatting to her

husband when we enter the room.

"There's not much happening," he says before we have the chance to introduce ourselves.

My eyes instinctively flick over to Paula to gauge her reaction, but she jabs him playfully in the ribs and lets out a low laugh.

"It's easy for you to say that," she says. "You don't have to squeeze a watermelon out of your…"

"We all know where they come out of," he interrupts. "No need to spell it out." There's a lighthearted humour to his voice, and I can feel the warmth in their banter.

"Next time you're doing it," she glowers.

He doesn't have time to argue about the biological logistics as she lets out a groan. Instantly he's beside her, stroking her hair gently and muttering low soft words that only she can hear.

Jade and I look at each other and smile.

"You're doing great," Jade says.

"See," she grunts. "I'm doing great."

"Of course you are," her husband says. "You always do."

When the contraction dies down, Jade nudges me forwards.

"How do they feel now? Are they getting stronger? More frequent?"

"Stronger, yes, a bit. How often are they, Sam?" she says, looking to her husband for the answer.

Sam shrugs. "I wasn't counting," he says. "I was just watching you."

Midwives and birth partners can serve similar roles, but sometimes I'm reminded of how differently we see things. I'm being trained to watch the clock, check how far apart contractions are, how long they last, how strong they are, and ultimately how long labour is taking. All Sam cares about is how his wife feels and whether everything is okay.

Right now, everything is fine.

Reassured, we head to room three to make our introductions to Cherry. She's on her own, filling in a crossword in what looks to be a gossip magazine. I've never really been interested in them, but they often get left on the ward when women have finished with them, so I end up flicking through them in the midwives' office. I know much more about the lives of Z-list celebrities now than I ever imagined I would.

"How are you feeling?" I ask.

"Bored," Cherry sighs. "I've read this mag twice and I've done all of the clues that I can on the crossword already. I'm not getting anywhere."

"No pains? Nothing happening?"

She shakes her head. "I wish."

Pain is a strange thing to wish for, but I've noted that when women are waiting to go into labour this wish is perfectly normal.

I smile. "Have you had any more loss down below?"

"Nothing," she says. "I just went to the loo, and my pad is dry."

I'm nowhere near as frustrated as Cherry is that her labour isn't starting yet, but I do feel a pang of disappointment. Even though looking after two labouring women isn't ideal, at least it would give me more of a chance of getting those deliveries. Every time I think about my PAD, I feel guilty, almost like I am using these women to make up my numbers. I hate thinking of it like that. I know that I need to prove, somehow, that I have had enough experience during my placements, but ticking off the numbers is never going to sit right with me.

Whatever happens today, I will give my best and think about the women, rather than the numbers. Having a student midwife as part of their caregiving team means that Cherry and Paula will be able to have more support and attention than they would if I were not here. I know that it's an unfortunate truth that sometimes there aren't enough staff around to be able to give every woman what she deserves. I wonder how I am going to feel about this when I am the qualified midwife, on my own with multiple women to support.

One day, hopefully not too soon after I qualify, I'll be allocated a student of my own. Me. Mentoring another student. The very thought of it gives me chills. I'm only just getting to grips with what I am meant to be doing, without having to mentor someone else.

That's a long way into the future. For now, I have to focus on one day at a time. Those days seem to be passing too quickly, and the empty spaces on my PAD are not being filled.

One day at a time.

Chapter Eleven

The end of term, and my enforced separation from Carl, comes around much too quickly. It's hard to believe I'm a third of the way through my final year already. I have the sneaking feeling that the next three weeks at home with Mum are going to feel terribly long.

Tomorrow Zoe will be driving Luke and I back to Portland, and Carl will be heading back to Leicester. Tonight though, tonight, I have him all to myself.

Or so I thought.

It's probably my own fault for trying to surprise him rather than making plans. I pictured an evening where the two of us would be here alone, get in a takeaway, choose a film, snuggle up on the sofa. I'm easily pleased, and this simple life, being together, is all I need to make me happy.

When I get home, Carl is up in his room. I don't know if it's because his room is up on the top floor with Luke's, and I don't need to pass by to go anywhere else, but I rarely go up there. My room is on the middle floor, across from Zoe's, so it's *en route* from the top of the house to the kitchen and living room. Today I make the trip up the extra flight of stairs and pop my head around the door.

"Hi," I say, hovering on the threshold.

He looks up, startled. "I didn't hear you come home. Hi, Violet."

There's a pile of books behind the door, and I struggle to squeeze into his room.

He stops what he is doing and kneels still on the floor behind his partially packed case.

"Alright?" he asks awkwardly.

"Er, yes," I answer, equally stiff and uncertain. I feel out of place here. "Do you want me to go so you can finish off?"

"You can watch if you want to, but it's not going to be very exciting for you."

He reaches behind himself for a stack of T-shirts and starts to unfold them, and then refold them into the case.

"Right," I say. This is not the evening I had expected us to have. "Do you fancy getting pizza later?" His face is blank, so I try something different. "Or Chinese or something?"

That feeling that I have done something terrible by not going home with him for the holidays is starting to resurface, and with it comes a wave of anxiety.

"Actually I said that I would go out for some drinks with the lads tonight," he says.

"The lads?" I ask.

When he first came to live at Tangiers Court Carl was fairly socially active, but for the past year he has pretty much spent his evenings here, at home, with me. He doesn't talk about any friends, and I can't picture who he means by *the lads*.

"Some guys from my course," he says, as though it is obvious. "A few pints, then probably hit The Basement."

I don't stop myself in time, and my face shows my disgust at the mention of the grotty nightclub. *The Basement* is in the town centre, not really a student bar, but the prices are cheap and it's open until four.

"You don't have to come," he laughs. "Don't worry."

Obviously, I didn't want to go there with him, I wanted him to be here with me. After letting him down over the whole Christmas thing though, I should suck it up and say nothing.

"Thanks," I say. "I don't think it's really

my scene."

"No," he agrees. "The girls in there aren't exactly like you."

My heart skips, and my brain races to unravel the meaning of the words.

"Oh?" I ask, trying to keep the emotion out of my voice.

He shrugs and turns around to grab another pile of clothes.

"Perhaps I should come with you," I say, pairing my words with a sweet smile.

"Ugh," he says. "Don't start that. I won't be late home. We can have breakfast together in the morning before I go."

"What time are you planning on leaving?" I ask. None of this is happening how I wanted it to.

"Depends when I wake up."

It's not a particularly helpful answer.

"Okay," I say. "Let's go out and have a breakfast date before you set off. You'll be starving on the way if you don't eat…"

"And I want to see you before I go. It's not just about the food, Violet," he says.

"I know. I mean, thanks. Er, you too. I thought I might see you tonight."

"We didn't make plans, so…I thought

you wanted to do our own thing."

"It's fine. Really. I wouldn't want you to miss going out with your mates."

"They aren't my mates," he says. "They're lads from the course, but yeah. Thanks."

He smiles and pats the floor next to him.

"Don't hover over there. Come and sit with me while I finish packing."

He reaches a hand up to guide me past the books, and around a pile of clothes to the space beside him. I try not to step on anything and settle down by his side.

"I've not got much more to do," he says. "It's more fun with you here though."

Watching my boyfriend folding his clothes as he packs to leave me for three weeks is far from fun, but being with him is preferable to being without him.

He puts his arms around me and gives me a long, steady hug.

"I'm going to miss you," he says.

"Oh gosh, you too," I say. "So much."

He draws back, and I think he is going to reach out for the clothes again, but instead he places a hand against my cheek, leans towards me and kisses me.

His skin is soft, and I inhale the scent of his aftershave as his lips move with mine. I want to remember that smell while we are apart. I want to take it with me. Really I want to take *him* with me. I don't know how I'm going to manage to be without him when we have spent every day together for so long. I don't want to think about that now. I don't want to think about the time we will be apart while he is here, still with me. I relax into the moment, wrapping my arms around him, drawing him closer.

After he has left, the house is cold and empty without Carl. I try to settle in front of the television, and I order the takeaway that I had planned for us to share. When the pizza arrives, I pick at it, take a few bites, and push the lid back down. I love pizza, especially tuna and mushroom, but tonight it tastes of cardboard. There's wine in the fridge, and though I rarely drink I pour myself a glass. Half an hour later I pour another, but neither does anything for me.

Zoe and Luke arrive home just after nine, and Zoe almost leaps out of her skin when she pushes open the living room door and sees me curled up beneath my blanket.

"Where's Carl?" she says.

Luke gives me a little wave as he passes by behind her and walks towards the kitchen. I raise my hand slowly to return the wave, and Zoe repeats her question.

"Where is he?"

"Gone out," I say. "It's nothing."

I gesture to one of the armchairs. I want her to sit here with me. I don't want to spend any more time on my own tonight.

"Nothing?" she says. "It's your last night together."

"It's only three weeks," I say.

I wish I hadn't said, because it sounds much worse now that I have spoken the words aloud.

"Where has he gone?" Zoe's voice is high-pitched and interrogative.

"Really, it's fine. He had arranged to go out with his friends."

"Didn't he tell you before? Or didn't he think that it might be a good idea to spend the night with you?"

"I was going to surprise him. I didn't plan anything, so he wasn't to know." Instead of feeling gloomy and grim I'm starting to get defensive and annoyed. My voice is rising. I don't want the conversation to go down this route. "Zoe, please. It's fine."

I see her eyes move to the wine glass beside me, still half-filled with the fruity red that she bought.

"If you're drinking it can't be *that* fine."

"How often do I drink? It's not like I'm an alcoholic! I probably drink less than every other student in the university. I think I'm allowed one or two glasses when I'm feeling a bit –" I stop myself before I say something that she can use against me. Still, she picks up on my words.

"Feeling what? Annoyed? Lonely? Let down?"

I didn't expect her to react like this. I thought we could chat and laugh and do what we would usually do with Carl not around. My cheeks are flaming with emotion. I want this to stop, right now.

As if sent by my guardian angel, Luke arrives at the door, awkwardly holding three mugs.

"Coffee?"

I reach out appreciatively and say, "Yes. Thanks. Perfect."

I drink the too-hot liquid too quickly. I want an excuse not to say anything else. I need something to shut me up and make sure I don't do or say anything stupid. I'm over emotional, probably overtired, and I don't want to take it out on Zoe.

She sinks back into the chair and lets out a hefty sigh.

Luke opens his mouth to speak, and she shakes her head, quickly and subtly, but I still see it. Instead of saying whatever he was about to he rests his and Zoe's mugs on the table and sits next to her in the second armchair. He looks over to the TV and flicks his eyes around the room for the remote control.

"I'm not watching," I lie. "Here."

I toss the controller over to him, underarm and cautious.

"Thanks," he says, and starts scrolling the menu.

I take a breath and speak. "Did you have a nice evening?"

Zoe pauses for a moment, looking at me, as if trying to decide whether to press me further or let it go.

"It was…great, yes. More than nice."

I grin, and it's genuine. I don't need to fake my feelings now.

"Tell me about it," I say.

And so she does.

When Zoe and Luke turn in for the night at half past midnight and Carl still isn't home, I decide to make my way to bed too. I want to be fresh in the morning to spend what time I can with him before he leaves. I wash my face and clean my teeth as slowly as I can, just in case he turns up, but he doesn't, and I go to sleep wondering where he is and what he is doing.

Chapter Twelve

Ever since I started working shifts my body has become used to waking up early. When I'm on the morning shifts I have to be at the hospital by twenty past seven, all perky and ready to work. My brain hasn't learnt to make the distinction between work days and off days, so I wake at six, and know it's far too early for anyone else in the house to be awake, let alone Carl after his late night.

It's still dark outside, dark and silent. My phone is plugged in to the socket beside my bed and I reach down to check the time and scroll through social media. No messages from Carl. A few exchanges on the group chat between Ashley, Sophie, and Simon, who were, apparently, still awake around two hours ago. I don't know how they do it. I might be a twenty-year-old, but I have the social stamina of a much older, much more tired woman.

There's not much else happening. I check the news, get diverted onto an article about Kim Kardashian, but it's all nonsense that I've already read about in the gossip magazines at work. I didn't care then, and I don't care now.

My feet are poking out of the bottom of the duvet, and the chill of the morning is nipping at my toes. I don't want to get up and bimble around the house on my own. It's too early for everyone else; it's too early for me. I pull my knees up, curl the duvet around me and reach over for my Kindle.

I've read a decent chunk of a festive-themed chick lit novel that I'm currently enjoying before I hear noise from Zoe's room. Hushed voices, quiet laughter, and the shuffling of bodies. Then, the thud of feet onto the floor, and steps padding across the room, through the door and onto the landing.

"Zo?" I say in a whispered shout.

She pushes my door open slightly and stands in the doorway, leaning lazily against the frame.

"Hey," she says. "Been awake long?"

I nod sadly and click-close my Kindle.

"I've nearly finished my Christmas reading already."

"At least you'll be in the festive spirit for my playlist on the way home," she grins. "Coffee? Toast?"

"Just coffee thanks." I shuffle up to a

sitting position. "I'm going out for breakfast with Carl."

She moves her head slightly in something that is almost a nod.

"Okay," she says. "Just coffee."

There's a thudding noise from Zoe's room, and she rolls her eyes, smiles, and turns to her own door.

"Sorry!" I hear Luke say, too loudly.

I want Carl to wake up and come downstairs, but I don't want him to be woken too early and be in a bad mood. These are our last few hours. I want us to both enjoy them.

Zoe patters downstairs and I can hear her singing to herself in the kitchen. It's not loud by any means, but if I can hear it from here, Carl can probably hear it upstairs. She's not the greatest singer, not that this bothers her in the slightest, and the Christmas number that she has chosen is certainly not the greatest song.

She's still singing when she pops my coffee mug onto the bedside table and motions for me to move my legs so that she can sit down.

"You okay?" she asks.

"Yeah. I'm okay."

"It's gone nine, you know. I'm sure it's fine for you to go up and wake him."

"Maybe," I say. "After coffee."

She gives me a semi-shrug.

"What time should we set off home?"

She changes the subject before we have any chance to teeter on the edge of an argument about Carl again.

"Anytime this afternoon. Mum is making lasagne for dinner, so I need to be back for that. You're both welcome to come over."

"That sounds great," she says. "It's been a while since I had your mum's famous lasagne. I don't know if Luke will be able to stop at one portion though."

"It is pretty good," I smile.

Already I can feel the tension leaving my body and ebbing away. Home. I can almost taste my mum's cooking and smell the rich, delicious tomato sauce. Maybe I should have that toast now after all.

Zoe looks around my room as she starts to drink her coffee.

"Have you packed?"

I make a sound that could mean yes, no, or maybe, and she raises an eyebrow.

"You're going to be busy once Carl wakes up. Have you got much to take?"

"I'll throw some clothes in a case. Nothing special. I got all the Christmas shopping delivered to Mum's."

Her face perks up at the mention, and I am sure she is about to start probing me for the details of her present when I hear sounds from Carl's room. There's a cough, deep and heavy, almost as though he's been smoking. Then I hear a scraping noise that I can't place, and finally a weak groan and the sound of his feet landing on the carpet.

I should have got up and got dressed. I could have saved time by getting ready, but I didn't think. I've just been lying here like an idiot, and now Carl is going to get dressed and expect me to be dressed too and…

"Calm down," Zoe says. "Calm."

I take a breath in, let it out, and nod in her direction.

"Thanks Zoe. I'm fine, really. I am."

If I tell her often enough, she might start to believe me.

If I say it often enough, I might believe it too.

Chapter Thirteen

Christmas goes exactly as I expected it to. Mum was so pleased to spend time with me, and I was happy to be home. After the first few days, anyway, when I started to relax, forced myself to stop thinking about Carl and let myself enjoy being there. It did start to feel like home again, with Mum bringing me hot chocolate at nine pm, settling back into the room that she hasn't touched since I started uni.

We talked, we played games, we ate, we drank, and we laughed. A lot. Still, I felt like something was missing. I've been so used to being with Carl. We've spent so much time together over the past year that his absence was inescapable. Is it possible to escape from something that isn't there?

I saw plenty of Zoe and Luke, and yesterday, the Saturday before the start of spring term, she drove us back here to Tangiers Court. So now it's late Sunday afternoon; Zoe and Luke are in the living room, and I'm upstairs, trying to concentrate on reading a book but distracted by the fact I know that *he* will be back any time now. I've

been thinking that since I woke up this
morning. I sat too long in the kitchen after
breakfast, though I knew it was too early for
him to be home. I listened for footsteps
outside the front door, for the jangling of
keys, but there was nothing. I tried sitting
with Zoe and Luke, but I couldn't focus on
the television or the conversation. Here I am,
buzzing with anticipation and rereading the
same page in my book over and over because
I'm not taking anything in.

Three o'clock passes, and then four. By five
I start to make dinner, and when it's cooked,
and he still isn't home I sit at the kitchen
table and wait. Finally, just before seven, I
hear his key in the door. I leap to my feet
and run out into the hallway. As soon as he
enters the house I throw my arms around him
and plant my lips firmly onto his. He's still
holding his case, and he lets it fall with a
thud onto the floor.

"Mmmf!" he mumbles through the kiss.

"I missed you!" I say, as I pull back to let
him breathe.

"I can tell," he replies.

He pauses to sniff the air. "Smells like

dinner."

"Yes," I say, breaking into a grin. "It's nothing really. Luke and Zoe have eaten. I waited for you though."

"That's my girl," he says, giving me a squeeze. "Come on then. I'm starving."

He walks down the hall into the kitchen, and I follow, pausing at the door to the living room to give Zoe a big smile and thumbs up. She probably thinks I'm nuts. She's usually right.

We've messaged and FaceTimed each other over the holidays but none of that is any real substitute for being together. I had that sneaking paranoia that I was messaging him too often or interrupting what he was doing. It's stupid, I know but I don't want to be that kind of girlfriend that always has to keep track on what their partner is doing. I don't want to come across as clingy and dependent, even if a tiny part of me does actually feel that way.

We almost trip over each other in the kitchen as I go to pull out his chair and he reaches out at the same time. I give a little giggle that splutters out of me involuntarily.

"Sorry," I say.

He smiles and sits in front of the place setting I've already laid out for him.

Perhaps this is learned behaviour, trying to woo him with food. My mum always used to cook for Dad when he was in a bad mood. I shouldn't downplay it like that. He was often in much more than a bad mood. Or perhaps it's more accurate to say that he was always in a bad mood and she used cooking for him as a way of mitigating his behaviour. It's not like that with Carl, of course. There's no *'bad behaviour'*; I do what I do because I love him, and I want to make him happy. This is one of the ways that I know of.

"Can I get you a drink?" I smile. "I got some beers, or do you just want a cola or something?"

"You really are spoiling me," he says. "Sure. I'll take a beer."

I nod and pull a chilled bottle of lager from the fridge and flick the cap off. Tonight, I've made curry. This is one of Mum's recipes. She cooked it for me last week, and now I am here, in my other life, cooking it for Carl. She calls it *Enthusiasm Curry,* because she puts everything she has into it. I found that hilarious as a child, and it still makes me smile today.

"What is it?" Carl asks as I place the plate in front of him.

"Curry," I say, stupidly. "Chicken curry. Not too hot."

He nods and stares at his plate. It's not a particularly attractive meal, but I know that it will taste amazing. Perhaps I should have played it safe and cooked up his favourite pasta.

I sit next to him, pulling my seat right into the table so I'm as close to him as possible without being in the way.

"Thanks Violet," he smiles.

"I missed you," I say, without thinking.

"Silly," he says. "It was only a couple of weeks."

I want to tell him that it was three weeks, and it felt like months. I want to tell him that I spent every day while I was away wondering if I should have gone with him to Leicester instead of spending the holidays with Mum. That each night when she went to bed at ten I would sit up trying to fill the time with anything other than my thoughts of him because I missed him so much that it almost physically hurt. That I envied Zoe and Luke being able to be together, even though I knew it was ridiculous to feel that way, and despite my couple-envy I was so happy seeing the two of them together.

Next year I have to spend Christmas with him, whether we stay with his parents, or with mine, I have to.

Then it hits me. Next Christmas I will be a qualified midwife. I will have a job and commitments. Chances are I will have to work at least some of the Christmas period. Babies don't stop being born because people want to spend time with their families. Women still need care and support, no matter what date it is. Perhaps I have missed my only chance, or at least my only chance for some time, of spending the holidays with Carl.

"Are you alright?" he asks. "Something wrong with the curry?" He peers into his meal jokingly.

"I missed you," I say again. Telling him that feels better than discussing next Christmas, a whole eleven months down the line. I've already been bouncing around like an overenthusiastic puppy, I don't want to overwhelm him with future plans.

His mouth is filled with another forkful of
the curry, so he gives me an awkward smile
instead of replying.

"So, how was your break?" I ask.

In between mouthfuls, he replies, "Okay,
thanks. It was Christmas."

"And your folks? Your family? Everyone
alright?"

He moves his fork slightly, as though
shrugging. "They're fine. Everything was
fine."

There's a strange tension in his voice, and
I don't know what to say next. He doesn't
seem to want to give much away about what
he's been doing. Maybe he is still annoyed at
me for not going with him.

"Did you get to see much of your friends
back home?"

"Christmas is over now, Vi. Let's talk
about something else."

"Right," I say, stunned. "I'm sorry. I
didn't mean to –"

He puts his fork down onto his plate, still
half-filled with the curry, and looks at me.

"No need," he says. "It doesn't matter. I
suppose I have had a long journey on a
packed train. It's not been the greatest day.

I'm tired; it's not your fault."

The tension drops from my body and I let out an audible sigh.

"I thought I had –"

"Hush." He places a finger against my lips, and I smile at the touch. "Really."

I want to apologise again, but I can't say anything. He takes his finger away and kisses me, his mouth warm and delicious.

Chapter Fourteen

I would have liked a few days of holidays with Carl before we both started our lectures again, rather than the few hours we actually had. On Monday morning I am back in uni, starting the penultimate term of my course. Although I haven't been tying myself in knots in the same way I have in previous years, the thought of the OSCE looming at the end of this term is not far from my thoughts.

I also have to knuckle down and get the bulk of my research project written up. It's a year-long module, but if I leave everything until the final trimester I'm going to make life ridiculously busy for future me. I had some time over the holidays to do some reading; not very festive, I know, but with Mum going to bed early and Carl being hundreds of miles away it seemed like the ideal opportunity.

We have the usual module introductions, and then I bundle along to the coffee shop with Simon, Sophie, and Ashley. I'm always either at home, at uni, on my placements or in a coffee shop somewhere. If anyone ever wanted to stalk me they wouldn't have to try too hard. I like routine, and I love latte.

"We'll be qualified midwives this year!" Sophie grins.

"Don't!" Simon says. "I need another three years yet."

Personally, I'm torn between thinking August can't come quickly enough and feeling exactly the same as Simon.

"We'll be fine," I say, trying to make myself believe it.

Ashley nods. "We have to be."

"Have you thought about where you're going to apply?"

Sophie directs the question towards Simon and me. No doubt she and Ashley have discussed it. There's something about the two of them being housemates that makes me feel somehow like an outsider. They bonded more closely from the start of our course, and they've had each other for support here and at home. Of course I have Zoe, and she's been amazing, but it must be great to have someone who understands the demands of our course and our placements. I'm almost envious of them, but I wouldn't swap Zoe for anyone.

Luckily, Simon is answering the question while I space out thinking about friendships.

"I want to stay where I've trained," he says. "Don't you?"

"Fliss is looking for a job in London, and I want to go with her," Sophie says.

"Nice," I say. "Things are getting serious then?"

Sophie nods. "Nearly two years together." The sparkle in her eyes when she speaks of her girlfriend is almost a cliché. "I'll go where she goes."

"That's good news for me," I laugh. As Sophie and I are based at the same hospital we won't be competing for a job if she moves away. A part of me would prefer to have her stay at St. Jude's though, so we have each other to turn to while we consolidate our practice.

"You're going to stay at the unit then?" she asks, smiling at my attempted wisecrack.

"I haven't thought too much about it," I say. "It's the nearest hospital to where I come from; my family is nearby, my mum. My friends are all round here. I don't want to leave."

My friends. These days that's Zoe, Luke,

and Carl. I couldn't imagine moving away.
Not ever.

"I moved as far from home as I could
when I came to uni," Simon says. "I feel
settled now. I'll probably stay here."

Simon has his placements in a different
unit, but if he wants to stay in town he might
decide to apply for a job at St. Jude's. On
one hand it's more competition for whatever
positions they have available; on the other
hand, I would love to work alongside him
and be able to chat with him over our
lunchbreaks. The more I think about
qualifying, the more I realise how much
ongoing support I might need. On paper, I
will be ready, as long as I have had my PAD
signed off. In reality, I know that I will still
have so much to learn when I start to
consolidate my practice.

Ashley is reading a garish flyer that
someone from Events has left on the table.
There's a lot happening on campus, but I
haven't participated in much of it at all. She
waves the flimsy paper in front of Sophie.

"Shall we go to this? Looks like fun."

"Fliss would love it; she's so smart."

"You're smart too," Ashley sighs. "Who

is that keeps getting the best grades in every module?"

"Only because I force you to stay up late and help me get them finished."

I love watching the two of them banter. They do remind me a lot of Zoe and me.

Now that she is with Luke and I am with Carl we don't get nearly as much time together as we could. Perhaps that's part of getting older, growing up and moving on. She will always be one of the most important parts of my life though, no matter what. I can't imagine ever being without her.

"Hey," Sophie says. "Are you up for it?"

I was miles away, lost in my thoughts, and my brain has to catch up with the conversation.

"The quiz?" I cast my eye over the details. Friday, five o'clock, the union bar. "Won't it be busy on a Friday evening?" I ask. My head fills with visions of the packed room, the noisy students, and the impossibility of having a successful slash fun quiz night.

"At five o'clock?" Simon laughs. "No one is out at five; that's why they're having the quiz then."

"It'll only be a couple of hours. We'll be done before the bar starts to fill up." Sophie does her best to try to convince him, but I can already see that he isn't going to need much persuading.

"I expect that's exactly the point," Simon says. "Get people in early to play the quiz and hope they will stick around for drinks later."

"When we win, of course," I smile. We. I said the word thinking of myself, Zoe, Carl, and Luke. Was Ashley planning for the four of us here to be a team?

"We will smash you," Sophie says, and I breathe a silent, relieved sigh.

I said it as a joke, but I am quietly confident that the Tangiers Court Four could take this quiz down. I might not be the smartest, but the other three are practically geniuses. As soon as I think it I start to wonder if that's the right way to pluralise *genius* and reaffirm my suspicious that I am not the clever one in the house.

"You three and Fliss?" I ask.

Sophie and Ashley nod in unison; Simon shrugs and says, "Sure."

"As long as I can persuade my

housemates, we will be there.”

The thought of doing something different is a thrill. We rarely go out, and if we do it's never as a foursome anymore. Not that I want to double-date or anything like that, but the four of us getting together for this quiz would be a break from the pressure of studying and a chance to dress up and let my hair down, literally.

Ashley folds the flyer and passes it to me. “Show this to your team. And make sure you point to that section.” She taps the upper side, where there's a bright yellow star with the words FIRST PRIZE £250.

“Too bad we will be taking that,” I say, and I tuck the leaflet into my bag.

Two hundred and fifty pounds might not seem a lot of money, but Christmas was expensive, and my student overdraft is always bursting at the seams. Every little helps, even split four ways.

Zoe is in lectures today too, so I have the chance to talk to her about the quiz on the way into town. It's a chilly day, the start of the second week of January, but not so cold that we can't walk it. Even though Zoe has a car there's nowhere to park on campus, and I would like to avoid travelling by bus as much as possible. It's close to freezing but walking and talking makes the journey feel like nothing at all.

"Well, it's different," she says. "Does it say what kind of questions there will be?"

I didn't even think about that. To be honest, I don't know much of the detail at all. I tug the flyer out of my bag and read it as we walk along.

"No. General knowledge."

"General. I wonder why they call it that. If it were that general we would know all the answers," she says.

"I'm hoping that you will know all the answers," I laugh. "I'm useless, but I thought it would be fun."

"It will give the lads a chance to show off, that's for sure."

I know that she is being playful when it comes to Luke, and I hope she has the same attitude towards Carl.

"Show off?" I press her further.

"I'm not sure he's as clever as he thinks he is," she smiles. "Not that he's not clever of course, I mean he must be to have landed you…" She pauses so I can give a sweet bow of appreciation. "…but there's a name for that isn't there? When, let's just say *slightly less intelligent* people think they're smarter than they are."

"That rules me out because I have absolutely no idea what you're talking about." I'm starting to wonder if I should have ever suggested this. I am going to be hopeless.

"Carl would know. Of course," she says.

"But he is studying psychology so he probably should know." I say it with a smile and Zoe shrugs.

"Do you think he will want to go with us? Carl, I mean." I can't conceal the uncertainty in my voice.

"If he doesn't, we can win without him," she says. She looks over to me to gauge my reaction, and then adds, "I'm sure he will want to come. Tell him there's money involved."

"I don't know," I say.

I thought it was going to be a fun night out, but the more I talk about it, the more I see the potential for disaster.

Chapter Fifteen

When we get back to Tangiers Court after our coffee and cake session I tell Carl about the quiz, trying to sound as nonchalant as possible. I don't want him to feel like he has to say yes. I'm not even sure I want him to.

"Sure. Sounds fun," he says, without hesitation.

He is smart, I know he is. Much smarter than I am. I'm afraid that I'm going to make an idiot of myself.

He gives me a tight squeeze, bringing me in close to his side, and I smile.

"The four of us will make a great team," Luke says. "Between us, we must know something about everything."

"Some of us more than others," Carl says.

He's grinning as he speaks, so I know it must be a joke, but I can't help but feel a quiver of anxiety shake through me.

"If there are any science-y questions you'll ace it, Vi," Zoe says.

She must have seen my discomfort, or maybe she only sensed it. All the same, she knows. She knows me.

"Maybe not everything science-y," I say.

"And I'm not sure 'science-y' is a word," Carl says, but he is still smiling as he pulls me so close to him that his hip jabs into me.

Zoe rolls her eyes playfully. "We'll be on the same team. We will be fine."

"Is there a prize?" Carl asks.

"£250 for the winners," Zoe says. "Not bad, even if we split it four ways."

"Nice," Luke says. "I guess I should revise."

Zoe laughs. "Revise? It's a fun quiz down the union, not your end of term exam. Oh, wait. Did you actually revise for those exams?"

"I did!" Luke laughs back. "A little bit."

"Little bit," Zoe mocks, affectionately.

"I passed," he says, with feigned indignance. She isn't having any of it though.

"Revise," she says again.

"Well maybe those of us who don't have the best general knowledge could brush up *a little bit* before Friday," Carl says, looking at me.

"We'll be fine," Zoe replies. "You can do some last-minute swotting if you like, but I'm only going for a laugh."

I thought that's what we were all going for, but it seems to have triggered a competitive streak in Carl. I'm starting to wonder what I have let myself in for.

On Friday afternoon, we get to the union bar at half past four; there are plenty of empty tables. It seems that Quiz Night is not quite as popular with everyone else as it is with Zoe and me. We have been bubbling about our team all the way here, and I can't help but feel disappointed that there's not a bigger turnout.

I look at Zoe and she reads my emotions perfectly.

"It's early yet," she says.

I can't see Soph and Ashley yet, so maybe she's right. More people might arrive before the start time.

Carl is board stiff beside me; I can feel the tension as I hold his hand.

"It's early," I repeat, to him.

He nods and sniffs. "Sure."

Luke eases the pressure by asking, "Shall we get some drinks in?"

Whether he was offering to buy a round, I don't know, but Carl says, "Great. Lager," and starts to move me towards a table in the centre of the room. I'd prefer to be tucked away by the wall or window, but I go with him, flashing an apologetic look to Zoe.

"Thanks, Luke. Do you mind? I'll just have diet cola, thanks."

Zoe and Luke look at each other and there's a trace of amusement rather than annoyance in their glance.

"No problem," Luke says.

Other students start to filter in, gathering in groups around the tables. It's much quieter than I have ever seen it in here, not that I have been a frequent visitor by any means.

Luke waves, and I follow his line of vision to see his course mates, Florin, Rajesh, and Damon. They haven't been round to Tangiers Court much over the past year, and Luke rarely goes out to meet them. I'm sure they must catch up over breaks, but it makes me all the more aware that Luke is part of our little bubble now: he, Zoe, Carl and I, together in Tangiers Court. I like it that way; I'm happy.

Luke has never shown any sign of wanting to do anything else, but sometimes, and more frequently of late, I'm starting to feel that Carl wants more time alone. Not because he doesn't want to be with me, or at least not just because he doesn't want to be with me. I'm not paranoid or possessive or anything like that, but I know that before he and I were together he would go out every weekend, and now he spends most of his time at home. I don't want him to get bored, or feel trapped, or…

"Hi, Vi." Sophie reaches down and gives me a hug.

"Oh hey," I say.

"You were miles away. Running over your general knowledge?"

"That wouldn't take me long," I laugh.

Sophie gives me a well-intentioned smile in return. She's with her girlfriend, Fliss, a mousey-haired northerner. There's no sign of Ashley and Simon.

"Oh, they'll be here," she says, as if reading my mind. "They wouldn't dare leave the two of us to defend the team name."

I let out a small squeaking noise and look at Carl. "We haven't thought of a name."

"What?" he says.

His attention must have been drifting too. He has no idea what we were talking about.

"A team name. Soph, what's yours?"

"The Deliverers," she says, proudly. "You know, like, because…"

"You three are midwives," Carl says. "Very funny. What about Fliss?"

"I'm outnumbered," Fliss smiles. "I couldn't think of anything better though."

I can't think of anything either. I know I shouldn't let this get to me, but thinking of an interesting, funny or cool name seems beyond me. I desperately hope that Carl makes a suggestion, because whatever he says, I am going with.

"Deliverers," Carl repeats. "Too bad you'll be delivering the win to us." He smiles amiably and the girls grin back.

"Good luck, team," Sophie says. "We're going to get some drinks and try to bag a table. Looks like they are starting to fill."

She's right. She and Fliss walk off and I look at Carl to see if he has any answers. Who know that the most important challenge would be choosing a name?

"TC," he says.

"TC?" I repeat. As soon as I realise it's a suggestion, I nod, and say the letters again, trying them out to see whether they work.

"TC."

"For Tangiers Court, obviously. It's the only thing we have in common, so that's what we should choose."

"The only thing the four of us have in common," I say with a smile.

"Well, yes," Carl says. "Team Tangiers Court is too long, and it sounds stupid, so we should be Team TC."

"That's fine," I say. When his expression appears less than pleased I change my wording. "That's great. It sounds great."

I could say that we should ask the others and have a democratic naming process, but I don't have any ideas of my own, and I don't want to waste the time that it will take for everyone to brainstorm, disagree, agree and end up choosing Team TC anyway.

"It's perfect," I smile, and I rest my hand on his leg beneath the table.

He looks amazing today. I have got so used to seeing him in the clothes he wears to lounge around the house that I forgot how well he used to dress to go out. I don't think I have seen him putting product into his hair for months, and this sweater must be new; I've never seen it before.

"You okay?" he asks.

I'm both nervous and excited, but I'm also happy. Happy to be out here with Carl, sharing something fun together, spending time and building memories.

"Super," I say.

I give his hand a gentle squeeze and he returns it. That can be our kiss. For now at least.

The quiz is a lot less difficult than I expected. Either that or I know more than I give myself credit for. Between us, Team TC get most of the answers right, and on those we don't, we are able to agree on an educated guess.

We have a moment of dispute when we say that the longest river in the world is the Nile, and the quizmaster tells us the answer on the card is the Amazon, but we're having too much fun to make a fuss.

When the scores are tallied, we have forty-five out of fifty. I'm almost certain that we will be the winners. We couldn't have done much more.

The quizmaster's system for working out who has won is to ask the room if anyone has scored fifty (no!), then forty-nine (no!) and counting down until someone eventually says yes. When no one has claimed forty-six out of fifty I know what is coming next. Or at least I think I do.

When the quizmaster shouts, "Forty-five," Carl immediately raises his hand and says, firmly, "Here."

Unfortunately, a team of lads that I don't recognise murmur amongst themselves, and then one of them raises his hand, his answers grasped tightly, and says, "Us too."

"Oh pants," I say, causing Zoe to fall into a fit of giggles rather than being upset that we haven't won.

"Do we have to split the money with them?" Luke says.

"Not likely," Carl says beneath his breath. "We have forty-five," he says, in the direction of the quizmaster.

"Ladies and gentlemen, it looks as though we have ourselves a tie-break situation."

The quizmaster reaches forwards and presses a button on the console, causing a dramatic section of music to boom over the speakers.

It's exciting, but I'm trembling in fear

rather than the thrill of how close we are to winning.

"Hey," Carl nudges me. "Get it together. We're nearly there."

I nod, straighten out my skirt over my legs without thinking about it, and sit up straight. It's like being back in school, ready to perform, desperate to impress someone, anyone. Most of all, back then, I wanted to impress my parents. Now, I want to show Carl that I'm not stupid. It seems to matter to me more than it should.

There's a pause in proceedings to let people refill their drinks, and to build the dramatic tension, I presume. For those who scored less than us and are already out of the race, there's the decision to be made as to whether they should leave now and get our before the rush starts to arrive, or whether to be glad they have tables, watch the rest of the quiz and bed in for the evening.

If we hadn't made it this far, perhaps I would be suggesting that we leave. As it is, I have another diet cola, and hope with all of my heart that the tiebreaker goes in our favour.

"It's going to be fine," Carl says. "We got this far. Don't say anything stupid and we will win."

It applies to all of us, but the comment is directed at me.

We blend into the busyness of the room, but I still feel like there are a lot of people staring at us: we are one of the two final teams, of course anyone paying attention is going to be looking at us.

"You okay?" Zoe asks the same question that Carl asked me earlier.

They both ask me it with higher frequency than they should need to. I am okay though. In general, I am mostly okay.

I give her the thumbs up and she returns the gesture. Carl shakes his head and picks up his fourth pint. Hopefully he hasn't drunk so much that he can't get the right answer to the final stage of the quiz.

Everyone that is staying settles back down into their seats, and the quizmaster plays a dramatic three note scale over the PA system.

"If you're ready, let's go straight ahead to the tie-breaker question. First to raise their hand and give the correct answer will be the winner. There's only one question, and this," he pauses, "is," he stops again, "it."

My mouth feels parched, and I reach out for my drink, and then put it down again. If he asks the question while my mouth is full, I won't be able to answer.

"Calm down," Carl nudges me. "It's okay."

I force a smile and lean towards him.

The quizmaster's voice is slow and steady, which is completely the opposite to how I am feeling. He asks the question, "On which organs are the adrenal glands located?"

I know the answer! Biology. Just my subject. I'm so thrilled that I forget to raise my hand, and instead, I whisper the answer loudly to the rest of my team.

"Put your hand up!" Carl says, stone-faced and stern.

I snap to attention and thrust my arm into the air.

"Team TC?"

"The kidneys!" I squeak the answer out.

"That's it. Well done, Violet," Zoe says.

"Good girl," Carl says.

"The kidneys," the quizmaster repeats.

"Team TC, that's the right answer.
Congratulations, you are tonight's winners."

I squeeze my fists excitedly into balls and punch the air.

My first instinct is to look over to Zoe. She is grinning and giving me the double thumbs up. I turn my gaze slowly to Carl, expecting to see him smiling back at me. Instead he is reaching for his drink, his eyes wandering the room.

"I did it," I say, unabashed.

He looks at me when I speak.

"Well done," he says calmly.

He pats my seat, and I sit back down. As soon as I settle, he reaches an arm around me and grips my shoulder, leaning to kiss my cheek.

"Well done," he repeats.

The thrill of the win is strong. Zoe and Luke are hugging, and I see Sophie and her team waving from their table. I wave back, grinning.

"Would the representative of Team TC please come to collect the prize?" the quizmaster says.

My excitement is stopped dead in its tracks. I don't want to have to get up in front of all these people and collect the money. Having everyone staring at me, watching me walk over, fumble the cash, and probably smash into a table or two on the way back is not my idea of a fun way to end a lovely evening.

Zoe leans across to me. "Hey. It's okay. I can go."

"Let me," Carl says, getting to his feet.

Zoe had already started to push her chair back so that she could stand, but when Carl speaks, she smiles politely and pulls herself in to the table.

"No problem," she says. "Make sure you bring it back," she adds, jokingly.

"I'm not going to skip the country with two hundred quid," Carl says, flatly, and he begins to walk over to where the quizmaster stands waiting.

Even though it was a team effort, and I won the tie-breaker question for us, seeing Carl collect the money makes me feel as though I am an onlooker, watching him win rather than being a part of it. I wish I had the confidence to get up in front of everyone, but that's simply not who I am. As he holds the cash, there's a ripple of dull applause from around the room. The clapping is for Luke, Zoe and me just as much as it is for Carl, but I find myself joining in with the crowd.

Zoe and Luke are looking around, enjoying the congratulations, and I feel like a spare part. I'm not good in public situations, I'm sure that's all it is.

As I try my best to relax and enjoy the victory, I feel a hand on my shoulder, and my body snaps to attention. It's only Sophie, with Ash standing beside her.

"You were great!" Sophie grins.

"I'd never have encouraged you to come along if I knew you were going to stop us winning," Ashley says, beaming.

The heat rises to my cheeks. "It was mainly the others," I say. "We were lucky to have that biology question at the end, really."

"I told her it was the kidneys." Sophie gestures towards Ashley.

"You! I knew it. Of course I remembered that."

"*Now* you remember."

The two of them look at each other in mock outrage as they exchange banter, and it serves to make me feel less self-conscious

and more comfortable. I'm immensely
grateful to them for that, but I don't say so.

"Have you had a good night?" I ask.

"We'll probably stay on," Ash says.
"What about you?"

It's already begun to get much busier than
I would like in the bar. I guess what Sophie
said was true: the organisers expect the quiz
teams to stay around for the rest of the
evening.

"I –"

I'm about to reply when Carl returns.
Sophie and Ashley are blocking his way
back to his seat, and they shuffle awkwardly
to the side to let him in.

"Well done, Carl," Ashley says. They've
only met each other a handful of times, but
she is always bouncy-friendly with everyone.

"Thanks," Carl replies. Without a shred of
modesty he says, "I knew we would win."

Ashley and Sophie both laugh as though
he is making a joke, but he remains straight-
faced. They let the laughter fade and look at
each other before turning back to me.

"I don't know," I say.

"Know what?" Carl asks.

"They were asking whether we were

staying on in the bar."

Carl looks up at the two girls. "You don't know Violet very well, do you? It's Friday night. She will be wanting to get home for her hot chocolate and whatever rom com is on TV."

That does actually sound a lot better than sitting here, surrounded by strangers, pushing my way through crowds every time I need the loo or want to get another drink. Although I probably shouldn't, I shoot a look at Zoe, and it seems to confirm to Carl that he was right.

"The pair of them. What are they like, eh?" Carl smiles at Soph and Ashley. "I think she will be going home."

I turn back towards him. I can read the meaning behind his words.

"You're staying out then?" I ask.

"You don't mind, do you?"

Of course it's a perfectly reasonable thing for him to want. I have no intention of stopping him, even though I would like to be at home, curled up on the sofa with him while I enjoy that hot chocolate and rom com. Even if I did want to persuade him to come home with me, it's not like I would start trying to talk him round in front of my friends.

"Sure. I'll head back with these two," I say, pointing at Zoe and Luke.

I want to ask whether he will be late, or who he will hang out with, but I don't want him to think I'm nagging him, and I don't want the girls thinking badly of me. For someone who thinks she's becoming more confident I certainly care a lot about what other people think.

Despite being thrilled about winning the quiz, as I expected Zoe and Luke are ready to go home too.

I lean to give Carl a kiss goodbye and he swerves so that I end up brushing my lips against his cheek.

"Not here." He says it firmly and I have a strange sense of déjà vu.

"Sorry," I say. "Later then. You owe me."

He smiles, but his eyes don't show any signs of sparkle.

"See you later," he says.

As we start to walk away, he calls out to me, "Be careful on the way home."

"Okay," I say, uncertainly. It seems like a strange thing to stop me for, but at the same time, it's sweet. He might be awkward in public, in a different way than I am, but he cares about me.

Chapter Sixteen

Carl didn't come home until after I had gone to bed, but on Saturday morning he is up bright and early, banging around in the kitchen. Because of my habit of waking early it's not a problem for me, but I hope that Zoe is up in Luke's room or they are going to be awoken too.

My eyes are still heavy, so I lie in bed, listening to the noises below, trying to make out what Carl is doing. He's at the oven, that's for certain. I can hear the clanking of pans on the hob. He is definitely making more than toast. That night out has either made him very hungry or very happy. If I am getting a cooked breakfast as a result, I don't mind which it is.

I'm back on placements on Monday; getting some quality time in with Carl this weekend is my only goal.

I don't have to wait long until I hear a gentle tap on my door.

"Violet," he says in a whisper loud enough to wake the next-door neighbours, let alone our housemates.

Pulling the cover off, I leap to the door

and open it. I would rather he had just let himself in, but despite having a strong, trusting relationship we still never enter each other's rooms without invitation. Living together this early in our relationship means that we need to have some boundaries, and it's working well so far.

He leans forward immediately and gives me a firm toothpaste-taste kiss.

"Good night?" I ask.

"Late night," he says. "Then I couldn't sleep, so I've made pancakes. You ready to eat?"

"Pancakes?" I say. That's not quite what I expected. "When did you learn to make pancakes?"

"Uh, over Christmas," he says. "They might not be perfect, but they look okay."

"Thank you!" The last thing I want is to sound ungrateful. I'm actually thrilled, just somewhat taken aback.

"Coming down?"

I can't help but be aware of all the noise we are making on the landing between my room and Zoe's, and now that he has mentioned the pancakes, I am suddenly famished.

"Try to stop me," I say, and he does a cute little dodge on the landing, playing along with the literal meaning to my words.

"No really," I smile. "Let's get this breakfast!"

True enough, there's a pile of fluffy golden pancakes on the table, and coffee for each of us.

"I don't know what I have done to deserve this, but it's amazing. Thank you," I say.

He ruffles my hair softly, then sits down next to me.

"Nothing," he says. "Nothing at all. I felt like doing something nice."

The glow in my heart is as warm as the pancake I fork into my mouth. I thought today was going to be a write-off, with Carl staying out so late last night, but it appears to be quite the opposite. The joy of winning might have helped him into this good mood; whatever it was, I like it.

The rest of the day continues in the relaxed, loving way that it began. We take a walk into town, through the gardens, and he's happy to wait while I stop to feed the squirrels. We sit for a while by the river that runs down the centre of the park. It's cold, but it's crisp. With no wind to chill us, the January day is near-perfect. We walk hand-in-hand, and my mind never wanders to thoughts of PADs, OSCEs or assignments. That can all wait.

Carl and I spend the entire day together, just the two of us. It's a rarity now, and I keep getting distracted thinking about how days like this don't come around often enough. That's part of my anxiety. It won't let me live in the moment and enjoy myself, I always have to be thinking about what could go wrong.

We have dinner at home and, as is our usual Saturday routine, we crash out in the living room with the others It's Zoe and Luke's turn to share the sofa, while Carl and I sit as close as we can on the armchairs. I don't mind too much. I can usually rest my head onto his shoulder and snuggle up to him despite the two thick chair arms between us. Tonight, he's leaning away from me, his knees tucked under himself, tapping away at his phone.

I want him to come closer, but he looks comfortable, and when I move towards him, he shuffles away. We've had a perfect day, and he has been so attentive and caring. I make myself comfortable on my own chair and try to let it slide.

"You okay?" I ask quietly. I don't want to disturb Zoe and Luke's enjoyment of *Cooking Queens*.

He nods, without looking at me, and points to the screen, as if indicating I should focus my attention there.

"We don't have to watch this," I say. "If you want to do something else, we can."

"I'm fine," he says. "Settle down."

Those two words have the opposite effect than that which I assume he intended. I don't feel at all like settling down.

I look over to Zoe and Luke to see how they respond to Carl's tone, but Zoe just smiles. Perhaps he didn't mean to sound as condescending and snappy as he did, but the Carl that I am sitting next to now is so different from the wonderful boyfriend that I spent the day with.

"What's wrong?" I press.

"Violet," he says, a little louder this time. "Seriously. Give me some space."

This doesn't make any kind of sense. He

has flipped his attitude towards me a full one-eighty since we were out earlier. The pancakes, the walk, they were so lovely, and now he doesn't want me near him.

"Okay," I mumble, but the way he spoke to me is needling into me too deeply for me to ignore.

I can't get comfortable. I want to *settle down* and have a relaxed, cosy night, but this is the opposite of that.

I pick up my mug from the side table, slip my phone into my pocket and take myself off to my room. Perhaps we both need some space, even if I don't know why. He might have used up all of his emotional batteries, being with me all day and being so wonderful. I know he put a lot of effort in, maybe he has earned some time alone. It must be difficult, living here with me, unable to get away.

I must have been upstairs all of five minutes before my phone beeps. Zoe.

You okay? Coming back down? xx

I don't want to be in Carl's way, and I definitely don't want to create tension, so I send a quick reply.

I'm fine. Little headache. xx

Zoe's response is a sad face emoji, and then a second text.

Need anything? Paracetamol? Water? xx

I should have known that her caring side would kick in. Why did I make up such a stupid lie?

Just overtired, I think. Thanks though xx

It's probably true. I've had a long, busy day. Taking to heart what Carl said is understandable. I'm overreacting.

Let me know if you need anything xx

I reply with two kisses and lay my phone onto the bed beside me.

I could be overreacting, but there's a niggling doubt inside me. I have the feeling that something is wrong. I've found recently that I am developing a sense for this kind of thing. I think it's something to do with the course. It's a kind of hypersensitivity, picking up on the tiniest signs that something is not quite right. On the wards, this is helpful, but here, at home, with my already anxious mind, it feels quite the opposite. When things are good, I make them bad, when they are bad, I turn them into disasters.

Carl has done nothing wrong, and I have enough to worry about with the things that I was not thinking about earlier, my exam, my assignments, and my placement. I should focus on those, and not try to create problems that don't exist.

And I really shouldn't start lying to Zoe.

Chapter Seventeen

On Sunday I try to play it cool, give Carl some distance, and even spend some time with my head in the books. Being together is one thing but being together too much is another. As far as I'm concerned, I could spend my every waking hour with him and still want more, but I understand that it could make him claustrophobic. He's always needed more space than I have, but lately his desire for distance is increasing.

Despite wanting to be with him, I'm almost grateful that I start back on my postnatal ward placement this week. I'll be out of the house for three evenings, which should give us the right balance of time alone and time together. It's perfect really. Being on placement doesn't allow my brain the time to mope about not being with him when we have those hours apart.

Frustratingly, I have a day off on Monday, but on Tuesday morning I am back to the ward. Much as I love my postnatal placements I'm not filled with enthusiasm for this block. I have four weeks here, and then three on antenatal before the holidays.

It's not long, not long at all considering this is my last placement in the Margaret Beresford Unit before I qualify. Am I ready? I'm about to find out.

My postnatal ward mentor, Geri, gives me the customary welcome back to the ward and gets straight to the point.

"I'm going to give you these two women and their babies to look after, okay? You can take handover from the night staff, introduce yourself and do everything that needs to be done."

She looks at me as though it's a done deal, not up for discussion, and knowing Geri, that's just about the long and short of it. Everything that Geri has done for me during my placements with her has been for my own benefit, even though I may have questioned that at first. If this is what she wants me to do, she must believe that I can do it.

My stomach is a tangled knot, but I nod. I have Geri as my safety net. I have the whole team. That's the thing with midwifery, even though you might be responsible for an individual woman, child and family, there are always other people on the team that you can call upon.

I repeat this thought to myself as I say, "Sure," and give Geri a smile.

It's been over a year since I was last here, but everything is fresh in my mind as though it were yesterday. The sound of the chatter, the women talking, the occasional cry of a baby, the voices of the staff; it all creates a pleasant hum. The tall windows let the spring morning sunshine fall into the middle of the Nightingale ward in a lemonade coloured wash. Everything feels good. I feel good, and I realise that I haven't felt this way for a while.

I'm thinking about the day ahead, planning the routine in my mind. Take handover, introduce myself to the ladies, work out if there's anything they need straight away before they have their breakfast. Check the babies have fed overnight, don't forget that. Eight o'clock, after breakfast, we do the drugs round. It's usually a one-midwife-job, apart from those meds that need to be signed for by two members of staff, but I, or one of the other students on the ward if there are any, accompany the midwife that's doing the round. I may have passed my medicines management module last year but it's an ongoing learning process. There are always new things to find out about.

After the drugs round I have the rest of the morning to carry out the daily checks, chat with the ladies, and do whatever else needs to be done. By then it will be lunchtime, almost time to go home. Time passes quickly when you're busy, and on the postnatal ward most days fly by.

Today I've only got two women and their babies to look after. When I am a qualified midwife, I could have half of the patients in the ward to care for. There's a big difference, and I know that Geri is only testing my ability to organise my workload.

Once all the rounds are completed, I stop at the bedside of the first of the women. Jane Judd had a Caesarean section two days ago and she's been tucked away in a side room with her baby. Clinically, she's fine. Her wound is healing well, the baby, a boy called Jasper, is feeding well, and everything seems normal.

"How are you feeling this afternoon?" I

ask.

"Bored," she says. "Stuck in here on my own, away from everyone."

"We try to room anyone that's had a Caesarean in a side room, so that you can get enough rest and, well, you have your own bathroom here."

"I'd rather be with other people," she tells me.

Although her vitals are all normal, there's a pale dullness to her face.

"I'll see what we can do," I say.

There are spaces on the Nightingale ward' it would be easy to transfer her.

She doesn't smile.

"Okay, thanks," she says.

I have a niggling feeling, one of those instincts that I've been developing while I've been training here. Something feels off. I don't know what it is, but I haven't been wrong before.

"Is everything else alright?" I ask. "Is there anything you'd like to talk about?"

She picks up a magazine from the side table and starts to flick through it.

"No, no," she says.

Her eyes are moving over the page, but it

doesn't look like she is reading. What it looks like is that she is pretending to read.

"Are you getting enough sleep?" I ask. I want her to tell me what's troubling her, because I am fairly sure now that something is. What I don't want to do is to pressure her and force her to shut down.

"When he lets me," she says.

Her voice sounds as though she is trying to make it sound light and happy.

"I have some time spare. We could bath him, if you'd like to?" I suggest.

"I don't want to bath him; I just want to rest. I want a break from him, that's what I want."

The words come out before she even realises she is saying them. As soon as she has spoken, she raises her hand to her mouth, dropping the magazine onto the sheets.

"It's okay," I say. "It's okay."

Before I can say anything else, she is sobbing into her hands, and I'm reaching over to offer a hug. She accepts it, and rests her head against me, letting the tears out.

"How long have you been feeling like this?" I ask, in a soft voice.

Did I miss the signs earlier today? This

isn't the first time I have been in the room.

"It, I don't know, it just came over me, all of a sudden. Maybe it's been building up. I feel so useless. I can't do anything for him. I want to, but I'm…I'm useless."

She starts to sob again.

"You're not," I say. "You had major surgery. You've been through a lot."

She nods, but her expression doesn't reflect that she believes me.

"Let's have a chat. I'll get you a brew and we can sit here and talk for a while, okay?"

"Okay," she agrees.

It's a good place to start.

The sun is still shimmering when I exit the double doors at the front of the unit and make my way to the bus stop. It glints off the car windows like sparkling diamonds. I know I have done something worthwhile today. I wanted to be a midwife so that I could make a difference for women, and I feel like I genuinely have. Jane might have a long way to go, but she will get there. She'll have whatever support she needs from the team on the ward and beyond. That really is a good place to start.

Chapter Eighteen

When I get home, the house is silent. Zoe is on placement this week too. Our practice blocks don't always coincide, but this week we have an overlap. It's strange to imagine her as Zoe, the student teacher, rather than as Zoe, my best friend. I wonder what she is like in the classroom. I know that Student Midwife Violet is a bolder, more confident version of me, but I can't imagine Zoe having to change anything at all to be a great teacher. She always knows what to do and say, it all comes naturally to her. She's cool and calm, and I'm sure she can handle anything. Perhaps I'm like that too, when I'm in the hospital. Maybe that's how people see me.

I flop onto the sofa, flick on the television, and open my phone. I don't think Carl is still in lectures, but they seem to change every week, and I can't keep track of them. It's tough being on a course where we have lectures five days a week, but at least it's easy to work out where I am. Lecture block or skills lab, simple. Wherever he is, he hasn't messaged me. There's no reply to the last text I sent at lunchtime.

The TV is tuned to the last channel we all watched, but instead of last night's *Medical Dilemmas* it's a crazy game show called *Talk Me Through It*. Couples take turns trying to explain to the other person how to do something. The first person sees only the instructions, and the second sees only the things they need to make whatever it is that the first is trying to describe. I could just imagine Zoe and I on the show. She would be hilarious. I'd be completely useless of course, but that's all part of the fun.

It's unusual but not unpleasant to be on a placement day where I'm not knackered. This is the start of my block of clinical practice and I know it will catch up with me after the first few days. It would be even better if my boyfriend were here for me to spend the evening with though.

My phone is still in my hand, but my attention is all on the TV. There's a buzzing sensation within my grip and I almost drop the phone in surprise. I had planned to text Carl and I almost expect to see his name on the screen.

It's not him though, and it isn't Zoe. It's a

message on the group chat that I'm on with Sophie, Ashley and Simon. I could have guessed without looking if I had waited, because the first buzzing is followed by a series of other incoming messages and their accompanying vibrations.

I click my phone and read through, still keeping an eye on the television.

Unsurprisingly I can't concentrate on both things at once, and I try to turn my focus to the TV. It's getting late though, and all I can think about is where Carl could be and why he isn't home yet. He's usually back around the same time every day, like clockwork. He knows when I usually eat, and he knows I usually make dinner for him too.

I message him again.

Are you on your way home? xx

It's gone six o'clock, and I thought he would be here by now. He still hasn't replied to the message I sent earlier. I'm starting to think that something could be wrong.

I don't have time to dwell too much, as the front door rattles open and Zoe clatters in.

"Alright?" she says, peering into the living room.

"Yeah," I say. It sounds unconvincing, even to me.

She pauses for a moment, slides her bag into the room, then says, "Hold up. I'll get the coffee."

I give a thumbs up and a smile, and turn the volume down on the television in preparation.

Within five minutes we are cosied up, each with a brew in our hands, deep in conversation.

"So what's happened?" Zoe asks.

"I don't know," I say, honestly. "He seems kind of off. I can't put my finger on what it is, but something doesn't feel right."

Zoe sits silently for a moment, and I'm about to start talking again when she finally leans back and speaks.

"Are you sure this isn't your anxiety talking?" She says it kindly, and in a way that I can't possibly interpret it as a criticism.

The thing is with Zoe I always know she has my best interests at heart. She's on my side, not that there are sides. Not that there's some battle stirring between Carl and me. It's probably nothing. She's probably right.

"You're probably right," I say.

I mustn't look sure of my words because
Zoe raises her eyebrows and shakes her
head.

"I'm not saying it's definitely that, Vi, but
think about it. You went out at weekend.
Everything was fine, wasn't it? Has he given
you any reason to feel this way?"

It's my turn to pause for thought.

"Not specifically," I say, drawing out the
word.

"But? There is a 'but', isn't there?"

I nod. "You know when you have that
feeling, and you can't shake it?"

"Like when I went on that date with Billy
Bell?"

She shudders for effect. She's been pretty
lucky with dating, but that one, that's a story
for another time.

I remember only too well.

"Just like that."

Now Zoe nods, taking a mouthful of her
brew. A serious look settles on her face.

"Maybe you're right then."

When she says the words I know they are
not what I wanted to hear. I wanted her to
tell me that everything is going to be okay
and that I am imagining things.

Perhaps I should have grasped at that lifeline she threw me and clung to the idea that my stupid anxious mind could possibly maybe be playing tricks on me. I don't want to be right. I don't want there to be something wrong.

"Do you think so?"

My voice has morphed to a husky whisper. I don't want to say the words, because I don't want to hear the answers. I don't want to believe that there could be something *really* wrong.

She sets her coffee cup onto the coaster and raises her hands.

"Vi, I don't know. It's hard being on the outside looking in. I see the two of you together and you look happy, but I know that doesn't mean that you are."

"It's not that I'm unhappy…" I start to say.

"You were unhappy enough to need to talk about it," she says. "I'd say that meets the definition."

I let out a heavy sigh. "Look at us. We should have better things to talk about, shouldn't we?"

"We should, and we probably do, but

right now I want to listen to you talking about what is on your mind. There's nothing wrong with sitting with your best friend, drinking coffee and talking about relationships. It might not be what the glossy magazines think we should be doing, but it's the reality of life, isn't it? Girls…women…want to understand their partners."

"Or at least understand their own lives," I say.

"Yeah, that too," she agrees. "But you have that sorted, don't you?"

"Do I?" I'm genuinely surprised by the idea.

"Sure! You're almost twenty-one and you already know exactly what you want to do with your life. That's quite something."

"You too," I say, as if trying to mitigate my togetherness.

She shrugs. "We are both impressive then. We have somewhere decent to live, we have great career prospects, and we are both healthy and –" She pauses and looks as though she is thinking about something.

"What?"

"Oh, you know. I forget sometimes, about

your anxiety. You've been on top of it for so long…"

"On and off," I correct her.

"The past eighteen months or so, you've been better than you have in years."

"On and off," I say again, and this time she shrugs and nods in acquiescence.

"On and off," she repeats. "But still, things are, in general, pretty good."

"So I shouldn't waste my time worrying about Carl?"

"I'm not saying that. It's obviously bothering you, so seeing as you are in a good place apart from whatever is going on between the two of you, perhaps you should talk to him. Clear things up."

I can't help but think about this time last year, when Zoe had recently started dating Luke, and she and I seemed to be drifting apart. Then it was Carl that I turned to for advice and support. He was there for me. He listened to me. He told me to talk to Zoe, in much the same way that she is telling me now. I let things stew in my mind. The tiny seeds of doubt and worry start to sprout into tendrils of anxiety that invade my every thought. It's almost as though I need

someone to give me the push, every time I
am feeling uncertain, to go ahead, to work
through my problems rather than letting
them overrun my mind.

Chapter Nineteen

I have it in my head that I will talk to him when he gets home. When he arrives, bends to kiss me, and I feel the same warm wooziness that I have been feeling for all these months I can't bring myself to ruin it by talking about problems that might not exist. Things appear to get back on track. We do the same things that we have always done, and everything seems normal.

It must have been my imagination, I tell myself. My imagination protests and puts the blame squarely onto my anxiety, and I can't help but agree. This is the most serious relationship that I have had, and it's a lot different from the casual teenage dating I have done before.

It's almost as though I was playing at being girlfriend-boyfriend in the past, and now I am deep into the role and I never really had time to prepare myself. Even though I was single for quite some time before I met Carl, it's almost as though I didn't spend enough time growing from a teenage girl into a young adult woman. I didn't have time to get to know myself before I got to know him. Somewhere along the way, a piece slipped out of place, and I've not been able to function at full capacity since.

My need to make people happy, and to put others before myself is what drew me into midwifery, but when I apply that to a relationship, instead of appearing caring it comes across as clingy.

I have so much to think about that worrying about my relationship is the last thing I want to do. I've noticed though that the more problems I have with Carl, the more time I spend with Zoe. She always makes time to talk to me now, especially after I told her how I felt last year when she had just started dating Luke and I was feeling lonely and vulnerable.

Because I didn't want to sound completely self-centred, I didn't use those words. Making Zoe feel guilty about not spending time with me because she wants to be in a relationship and have time with her boyfriend too would be beyond the pale. I have to handle my own emotions; I have to deal with my own relationship issues, even though I know that Zoe is there now

whenever I need her, whatever I need her
for. Our friendship is solid, no matter what
happens.

So, I carry on. I try to put my doubts to
the back of my mind, focus on my studying,
getting through my placement and not letting
my mind get carried away with itself. It
seems to work. In fact, it's working
absolutely fine right up until it isn't
anymore.

The evening before my OSCE, Carl offers to
give me some space so that I can revise. Last
year he offered to run through the scenarios
with me, but there has been no suggestion of
that this time around. I've practised with
Zoe, and got together with the gang from my
course though, and now all there is to do is
to make sure I know absolutely everything
about the potential scenarios that I might get
tested on. Simple, right?

The exam will focus on emergency
situations like postnatal haemorrhage, what
to do if the baby's shoulders get stuck during
delivery, or if the umbilical cord pops out of
the birth canal before the baby is born. For a
simple, natural life event there's a lot that

can go wrong during childbirth. It's part of my job to know how to respond, and I need to know that off by heart.

One of the first steps in nearly all the emergency drills is to call for help. Pull the emergency bell. Shout. Get someone else in there. I will have to know how to handle the situation, but I won't be alone.

I've written all of the steps for all the emergency situations onto postcard-sized cards, and I am drilling myself on them over and over. There are mnemonics for some of them, to help me, and all the other midwives, to remember what to do and what order to do it in.

I'm running through the card that I've headed "Shoulder Dystocia" for what I am sure is the hundredth time when there's a buzzing from beneath the duvet at the bottom of my bed. I instinctively reach down, fumble through the cover, and pick up the phone.

As soon as I feel it in my hand, I know it's Carl's and not mine. It's lighter, and slightly larger, not so much that it's visibly noticeable but I can feel the difference. He must have left it by mistake when he went out earlier; he's never usually without it.

I should put it down somewhere that I won't knock it onto the floor, and leave it alone. It's too late though. I've already looked at the screen.

Are you coming over tonight? xxx

The five words alone wouldn't necessarily have grabbed my attention. Carl has friends, even though he rarely goes out with them anymore, I know that he texts his mates and spends time with them sometimes now. Not often, but sometimes. It's normal, it's healthy, and it's probably something that I would be doing too if I didn't live with my own best friend. Zoe and I have our weekly mate date and impromptu trips out when we both have the time and opportunity. What kind of girlfriend would I be if I wanted Carl to stay at home with me every night?

Are you coming over tonight?

It's the three kisses at the end of the text that reach into my chest and grip my heart with a cold, icy hand. I almost expect it to stop beating; I can barely breathe. I'm glad I am already sitting, because my head is dizzy, and my legs are trembling.

Of course, the name of the sender is also

on the screen, or at least the first letter of the name of the sender. Carl has stored the name in his phone as simply '**B**'.

B

Who the heck is '**B**'?

I stare at the screen, reading the five words and taking in the three little **x** marks.

His phone is locked, but I know how to open it. He doesn't have a passcode, and unlike my phone he doesn't need to press his thumb against the pad to open it. There's a pattern, a swipe across and then diagonally down from top to bottom; if I run my finger over the screen I can read the other messages that he and B have sent to each other.

It could be completely innocent. Some people add kisses to every message. Ashley is always throwing them into the group chat. Zoe and I exchange them all the time.

I sit up and my revision cards tumble onto the floor. Normally I would scoop them up straight away, get them back in order and focus my attention on the task in hand: revising for tomorrow. That's the most important thing right now; that's what I should be doing.

Are you coming over tonight?

Coming where? Who are you B? Why do you want my boyfriend to 'come over'?

I have a half-drunk spinning sensation in my head that I can't shake. The phone is like a brick in my hand, weighing me down. I want to drop it, but I hold on, looking at the screen, wondering whether I should open it up and see what else is hidden inside.

Zoe is out with Luke. She would know what to do. She will know.

I put Carl's phone gently onto the bed beside me, as if I am afraid that it will run away if I move too suddenly. Instead of opening his phone, I open my own and tap out a message to Zoe.

I need to talk to you xx

Typing the kisses hits my stomach like a punch.

I don't stop to think; I click send and wait for Zoe's response.

I expect her to text back, but instead of the chirping of a message, my phone rings.

"Hey, what's up?" she asks as soon as I answer.

She sounds like she is trying not to sound worried. Poorly concealed concern filters through her voice.

"I saw something, and I don't know what to think."

I explain about the message, almost stuttering and stumbling over my words as my emotions take over.

"I thought you were revising," Zoe says, before she even starts to respond to what I have told her.

She's buying time, thinking about what to tell me, I know it.

"I was. I have been. That's kind of gone out of the window now."

"Well, you need to get it back," she says. "Unless you're going to break into his phone and read through his messages there's nothing you can do apart from wait."

I hear her sigh and then she asks, "Do *you* think he could be seeing someone? Is that what this is?"

"No," I say. It's my instinctive response, but if I really believe that why is the message affecting me so badly. Things have not been perfect between us, but that's no reason for me to think that he would be with someone else. "I mean, maybe." I pause, and then say, "Yes."

I can hear Luke in the background at Zoe's end, asking her what's wrong. She must look as shocked as I feel. She moves the phone away from her mouth and talks to him, quickly explaining, and then comes back to me.

In the distance, I hear Luke say, "Do *not* read his messages. It's only going to lead to bad things."

"I think Luke's right, Vi," Zoe says. "You need to talk to Carl. Give him chance to explain what's going on. It could be nothing."

"It could be nothing."

It could be something.

It could be everything.

Chapter Twenty

When I say goodbye to Zoe, I take Carl's phone, place it into my drawer and shut it away. I don't want to see it or think about it; at least I can do something about one of those things.

It's true that our relationship has felt different recently, but isn't that because of the stress of our final year, just like we said it was? I still want to believe that everything could be okay. I want to believe that everything is in my head, but I have that sick feeling, that nauseating intuition that is insistently telling me that there's something going on.

Carl arrives home sometime after eleven. He stops in the kitchen below and I can hear him walking across the lino floor. He turns the tap, pours water, pauses, walks again. I am focused on every step he takes because all I can think about is wanting him to come up here so that we can discuss the message. That's not all I can think about. Not really. Despite everything, my thoughts are also focussed on how much I really do not want to open this can of worms.

Now I could play dumb and nothing would change between us. He would come into my room, kiss me, and everything would be exactly as it has been. As soon as I start to ask him about the message, things are going to change; I know it. Still, I have to do it. I need to know. Even if it is nothing, my over-anxious mind needs an explanation, or I am going to worry myself into a state.

Finally, I hear his feet on the stairs, and he pushes my door open.

"Hi," he says, walking across to me.

He perches beside me on the bed and reaches over to kiss me hello. I can't stop myself from withdrawing. I should have played it cooler, tried to act in a more natural way, but my anxiety has burst through to the surface and there's nothing I can do to conceal it.

"What's up?" he asks. When he pulls back I can see the hurt in his face, and I think for a moment about making something up instead of going through with the conversation I know we need to have. "I left my phone somewhere," he says. "I'm sorry that I didn't message you if that's what's wrong."

That's enough to tip me over the edge. If he hadn't mentioned the phone maybe the conversation would be calmer, but I feel so worked up that I lash out.

"Yes, you left your phone. You left it on my bed. You had a message while you were out from your friend **B**. Is there something you'd like to tell me?"

As openers go, I know immediately that it is a bad one.

Carl looks stunned, and then the anger breaks through.

"You read through my messages? What the hell do you think you're doing? What gives you the right to check up on me? Is that what you were doing? You don't trust me, so you decide to snoop around in my phone. One time I happen to leave it here, just one time, and you do this? What is wrong with you? Why would you do that?"

His voice gets louder and faster as the tirade of questions roll off his tongue. He's up on his feet now, standing by the side of my bed, looking down on me. I feel like a cowering mouse.

"No, I…"

He doesn't give me the chance to explain what actually happened.

"There I was thinking that you had an important exam tomorrow and you needed me out of the way so that you could revise. No. That wasn't it. You wanted me out of the way so that you could nose through my phone. And my room as well? Have you been up in my room going through my drawers? Checking through my pockets?"

Even though he is standing, he leans closely to my face and spits his words at me.

"Carl, stop," I say.

He stands deadly still, glaring at me. I shouldn't have said anything. I shouldn't have picked up his phone. I shouldn't have looked. It was innocent though, all of it was. I never intended for any of this to happen. Now I have ruined everything.

"What do you want me to say?" he asks. "Whatever I tell you, you seem to have already made up your mind. You think I've done something wrong; I can tell by that look on your face. When I come home you're usually all over me, and today you can't even kiss me. You don't have to say anything, that says it all."

He's right, of course. I saw the message and instead of giving him the benefit of the doubt I called Zoe, I didn't even consider that there could be an innocent explanation. Carl is my boyfriend, and I should have trusted him.

"I'm sorry," I say, quietly.

"What?" He sounds incensed, his voice booms in my face.

"I said I'm sorry," I repeat, as calmly as I can manage.

"You crossed the line, reading my messages. I can't believe you would do that."

"I didn't. I mean, I picked up your phone by mistake and I saw what was on the screen. I would never –"

"You accidentally picked up my phone and then you accidentally read my messages?" He laughs acidly. "Sure, Violet. Sure, that's what happened."

"You must have left it."

I try to explain, but when I speak, he cuts me off, stopping me from getting the words out.

"I never expected this of you," he says, shaking his head. "Accusing me like this.

173

Show me your phone. How about I read through your messages?"

"There's nothing in there. Nothing you'd be interested in. And I didn't read through your messages. It was only that one, on the screen. I never opened your phone."

"But you know how to, don't you? You've made sure of that. I've seen you watching me."

He looks at me for a response and I can only nod. My phone is on the bedside table, and he snatches it. Stupidly I reach out to try to take it off him.

"What? You don't want me to look? I thought there was nothing to see. If you've nothing to hide then I can look, can't I?"

I wish I had never started this, but I did, and now I am stuck in a bad situation that I don't want to make any worse. Even though I know there is nothing on my phone that Carl shouldn't see, my anxiety is building up to a point that I know I must look guilty regardless. I can hardly breathe let alone find the energy to argue.

"Yes," I say resignedly, and I flop back against the wall to watch.

"Open it."

He holds the phone in his hand so that I can press my thumb against the pad without being able to snatch it off him. I wasn't going to. I don't care. I can't fight him; I don't want to.

I put my thumb on the pad and as soon as my phone opens, he whips it away and starts to scroll through. Instead of moving so that I can't see what he is doing, he reads in a way so that I know exactly what he is looking at. He's trying to get some sort of reaction from me, but all I have is submission.

He flicks open my social media and runs through the private messages. There's a couple of exchanges I have had with other student midwives that I've chatted with online, and some threads about book swaps. His expression starts to change from anger to a bizarre amusement.

"Is this it?" he asks. "Is this your life?"

"What?" I stutter.

"Is this all you do? I mean I don't want to find that you've been talking to other guys, but I expected something interesting at least."

Something inside me snaps, and I sit up sharply.

"Give me my phone back." My face is poker straight and I am deadly serious.

He speaks back to me with the same sharp directness. "I haven't finished yet."

I reach across again, flailing for my phone, and he holds it away, out of my grasp, and gets to his feet.

He's moved on to my phone call log. I know, even though I can't see anymore. I know because the next thing he says is, "You called Zoe. As soon as you saw that message, you called Zoe."

He holds the phone out towards me, accusingly.

"Everything that happens, everything I say, everything I do, it all gets back to her, doesn't it? Do you have any thoughts of your own that you don't run by her first?"

"That's not fair, I –"

"Is it fair on me? Is any of this fair on me? What did she tell you to do? Did the two of you have a lovely little chat about how terrible I am and how I definitely certainly positively must be cheating on you?"

He throws the phone at me, and luckily it thuds into my abdomen rather than striking my face. Still, he has crossed the line, and I can't accept this.

I take a deep breath and try to make my words sound as calm as possible. "I have my exam tomorrow. I can't deal with this now."

"What's more important to you? Sorting things out between us or your stupid exam."

The words land like a slap and I recoil just as though it was a physical blow.

My instinct is to blurt out, *'You, you of course,'* but I pause and that's all it takes to tip him over the edge, if he wasn't there already.

"I knew it." He practically screams the words at me.

"Carl!" He turns to walk to the door. "Please. You are important. You are."

"I am important. I know I am. Just not important to you." He spits the words out. "You were the one that started this. You wanted this argument and now you've got it you can't handle it. You can't start accusing me of things and then expect to schedule an appointment to talk about it."

There's a tap at the door, and I hear Zoe's voice. I didn't hear her come home, and I wonder how long she has been able to hear what's going on.

"Everything okay?" She sounds hesitant, a slight tremble in her voice.

"Fine," Carl says. "We're finished."

Finished talking or *finished* finished? The question jolts through me, but I can't speak. My mouth has turned to useless jelly.

He pulls the door open and pushes past Zoe, his feet stomping on the stairs up to his own room. The second he is gone I bury my face into my hands and let the tears out.

Zoe runs in and sits next to me, her arms around me before her rear hits the duvet.

"Hey. It's okay. It's okay. What happened?"

I hear the door move and flick my eyes up to see Luke pushing it closed from the landing. He must have been behind Zoe, backing her up, being there for her.

I shake my head and snort back snotty tears.

"Come on," she says softly. "Hey."

Her hand smooths my hair in gentle strokes, and I rest my head on her shoulder.

"I've made such a mess of things," I say.

"So, he hadn't done anything wrong? He hasn't? What did he say? What was it all about then?" She pulls back to look at me and bites her lip. "I'm talking too much," she says. "Tell me what happened."

I give her the short version of events and she sits expressionless and listens. When I have finished she finally speaks.

"So he didn't deny it," she says.

I had missed that less-than-minor detail amidst my anxiety.

"Well, no," I say. "But he was so angry that I had been looking at his phone. I couldn't really keep asking."

She sighs and shakes her head. "And what was the shouting about? Does he know your exam is tomorrow? He must do. Are you ready? No, don't answer that now. Tell me why he was yelling at you. I just wanted to burst in here and…well, I don't know what, but Luke stopped me. He said, *'Be cool. Don't make things worse.'* Worse? I ask you. What's worse than someone yelling at my best friend. Well, I know…" She stops herself again and reaches out to wipe my tears.

"I don't care about my exam. I've messed everything up. I'm so stupid."

"Violet Cobham you are not stupid. You

are not. And the fact he is making you feel this way gives me even more reason to doubt him."

"She's probably just a friend, Zoe. He's allowed to have friends. It's not even a case of being allowed. I don't have the right to allow or not allow anything," I say through my bubbling tears.

"You have a right to expect him to be faithful and honest and not treat you like an idiot."

"I am an idiot," I mumble.

"You should go up there and sort this out. Ask him, straight up. Ask him what's going on. Find out who this **B** is."

It's the last thing I want to do, but I do need to finish my revision and there's no way I can even think about my exam with this hanging over me.

I tighten my lips and look at Zoe.

She gives me a reassuring smile.

"Whatever happens, you are going to be okay, Vi. I promise."

Even though my heart is beating out of my chest, I steel myself to get up and say the words that need to be said. As I push my hands into the bed to stand I hear Carl's feet on the stairs.

"Wait!" I call after him.

I get to the landing in time to see him opening the front door.

"Carl, please. Wait." I shout the words, and they sound so alien, so desperate.

He pushes the door and leaves the house without so much as turning around to acknowledge me.

I've really made a mess of this. I've ruined everything.

Chapter Twenty-One

When morning comes, Carl doesn't show for breakfast. Either he got up early to avoid me or he's hiding away in his room. Although part of me wants to talk to him, and to get some kind of reassurance that everything is going to be alright between us, there is also a part of me that is relieved that we don't have to go through another argument this morning. I have to get my mind focussed on the exam ahead of me.

I know it's going to be tough, and with Zoe on placements I'll be walking into uni alone. I force myself to think about drills and mnemonics, repeating them over in my head like particularly dull mantras, blocking everything else from my mind. It feels impossible. Carl keeps creeping into my thoughts. No, not creeping; the thought of him crashes in, like an uninvited party guest. Each time my attention drifts to him, I start running through another list, repeating it over and over until all I can think about is the exam.

I get to the skills lab five minutes early, just as I planned, and after the all-too-familiar wait in the corridor, my legs are like jelly when I walk into the room. This is it. My third and final OSCE. I have to pass. I have to focus.

I can't believe how easily I breezed through this last year. I was so confident then, so sure of myself and my knowledge. Now I feel completely unprepared. I did what I could last night, but the feeling runs deeper than that. I don't only feel unprepared for the exam, but also for the end of my course, for qualification, for practice as a midwife. There's a chance that my insecurity and self-doubt have been kicked up a notch after what happened last night, but there's also a chance that I really am not ready for this.

I try to smile at Zita to conceal my fear.

"Hi Violet," she smiles back, and it feels warm and reassuring. "You know Sarah and Amanda." She gestures to the second lecturer and the woman who will be standing in as a patient.

I nod. Thoughts of Carl and our stupid argument are cycling through my brain, pushing out all the things I need to remember for the exam. I can't think about him now. I can't let my brain wander to working out who B is and what she is to Carl. I have to stop this, right now.

It's so much easier thought than done.

"Hi," I say weakly.

Hearing my own voice makes me snap to attention. I reach up and straighten my collar, wipe a stray hair from my forehead and take a deep breath.

"Hello," I say again, and this time my voice rings out strong and steady.

My lecturer grins. "That's better."

She wants me to succeed. Sarah wants me to succeed. Even Amanda, the stand-in patient, who barely knows me, wants me to succeed. I have to want it too. I have to want it enough to focus, to put all of my mental energy into the here and now and ace this exam.

Once we have begun, everything starts to fall into place. I have drilled the mnemonics into my memory bank efficiently enough that I can pull out the information I need when I need it.

The first scenario is shoulder dystocia. It's not something that occurs often, and I haven't experienced it in practice, but if it does happen I'm going to need to know what to do. In a routine birth once the baby's head is born, the shoulders are delivered with the next push. The upmost (or anterior as we call it) shoulder slides beneath the mum's pubic arch and the rest of the baby follows in one, sometimes slippery, motion. In a small number of deliveries the shoulder gets stuck against the bone: that's shoulder dystocia. It's risky for the baby; being stuck in the birth canal can lead to nerve damage, brain damage, and even death.

This OSCE is not a paper exercise. The lecturers aren't testing our memory recall skills. They need to know that if, or when, we experience these situations in practice we know exactly what to do. Acting quickly and correctly can mean all the difference.

My mind flicks into gear as I respond to the scenario. My instincts kick in, and if Carl were to walk into the room now I wouldn't even give him a glance. This is how it should be. When I am in my uniform, with woman, all that matters is giving safe, supportive care.

When I leave the skills lab, I'm buzzing with

the thrill of knowing that I've aced the OSCE. I knew everything I needed to know, and I did everything I needed to do. Despite last night, the lack of sleep and the distraction of my row with Carl, I kept my head.

As soon as I think about last night, my mood drops an octave, and my smile turns into a frown. I've passed the toughest assessment on my course. I should be happy, but instead I'm walking home worrying about whether I even still have a relationship. That's without even thinking about everything that led to our argument in the first place. All that rowing and for what? It didn't achieve anything. I can feel the anxiety gripping me like a tight hand around my wrist, drawing me back from the happiness that I should be feeling. What's going to happen to us? What's waiting for me when I get home?

My phone buzzes, still switched to silent from the exam room, and I jump as I feel it vibrate against my side. I half-expect it to be him. I want it to be. I want some reassurance. Just a few words. *'We'll talk when you get home.'* Even something as formal as *'Hope your exam was okay.'* I'd take it. I'd take anything right now.

It's not him though. It's Zoe.

How did it go? xx

Of course it's Zoe. She's always there for me. No matter what. That doesn't stop me from feeling a little pang of disappointment as I read her name on the screen instead of Carl's.

I stop at the traffic lights, waiting to cross the road and tap out a reply.

Fab xx

I add a smiley face emoji, even though I don't feel much like smiling.

I send the message and turn my attention to the road. It's not quite rush hour, but the traffic is picking up and there's no way I'm getting across unless I wait for the green man to flash up.

I sigh and type a follow up.

Are you home? Have you seen Carl? xx

I stare at the words on the screen until I hear the rapid beeping of the pedestrian crossing. Shaking my head, I pop my phone back into my pocket without sending. What can she say that is going to make me feel any better? Nothing. Not by text message anyway. I raise my head, focus on the way forward and try to let myself enjoy the cocktail of relief and satisfaction from making it through the exam – without the side order of self-doubt and anxiety.

There's no sign of Carl when I get back to Tangiers Court, but Zoe runs to meet me.

"Tell me all about it," she grins as she ushers me down the corridor towards the kitchen.

There are already two mugs on the table, filled with fresh tea, and she's laid a plate of biscuits out as though we are having a party. I know she is trying to be sweet, but the strangeness or seeing them there is somehow jarring and I swallow my smile.

"Sit, come on," she says, relentless.

I can't help but return her smile, and I tuck my jacket onto the back of the chair and settle in front of my mug.

I'm aware of myself listening for signs of Carl's presence. I can recognise the sound of his footfall, somehow different from Luke's. Not heavier, but more defined. Firmer, maybe. It's something I've become tuned in to. Now, there is only silence. No Luke. No

Carl. Zoe and I are alone here, the two of us sitting beside each other in our home.

I'm about to speak when Zoe edges in. "Tell me about your exam."

I'm sure she knows that I want to talk about last night, that I want to thrash out the details of my argument with Carl and look for some suggestions on what to do next. Instead of pushing it, I take a biscuit and start to tell her about the OSCE.

The mugs are emptied and filled again. I stop myself from eating more biscuits because it's nearly half five and time to be thinking about dinner rather than snacking. Still, it's just the two of us. We go from talking about my exam to discussing her day and the portfolio she's putting together for her course. Although we are studying for different career paths there are many similarities between what we are doing. We've always been that way, the same in so many aspects, but different enough to be our own individual selves.

Her face glows.

"So, I went to my supervisor and she said she would have done the same thing," she laughs.

An aura of confidence emanates from her as she tells me about how she handled a particularly tough situation in a class this week.

"You have to go with your gut," I nod, understanding the principle, even if I don't understand the exact situation. "As long as your supervisor agrees you must be on the right track."

I haven't taken the time I should have to reflect on how much Zoe has changed, developed and grown since we have been at uni. Looking at her now, I can see it. She's a little older, of course, but she is so much wiser, so confident and comfortable in who she is and what she is doing.

The thought catches in my throat, and without saying anything I lean over and throw my arms around her, squeezing my best friend in a tight embrace.

"Hey! What's that for?" She laughs and encircles me with her arms too.

"I just wanted to. I had to," I say, pressing my face into her hair. I know she can hear the smile in my voice anyway. "You're…I don't know. It sounds silly. I'm proud of

you. It does sound silly, doesn't it? But, I
am. Look at you, so…together." I pull back
and look her in the eye. "You're going to be
an amazing teacher."

"Oh Vi." I swear that's a tear in her eye.
"You silly, silly…" She shakes her head but
doesn't stop grinning. "I look at you and I
think exactly the same thing. Everything has
come easily to me. I haven't had to cope
with any of the things that you have, not
now, and not before we got here. My life has
been an easy ride. Think about how you
were back when you did your first OSCE.
You've fought back and here you are
breezing through your exam today."

I get an instinctive blush of shy humility
and have to look away.

"Own it. Own your success."

She's like my personal cheerleader. This
started with me complimenting her, and she
turns it around every time to make me feel
good about myself.

I nod. "I own it," I say, "but you're going
to have to take some of the credit."

She shakes her head resolutely. "I'll take
the credit for my success, and I absolutely
acknowledge that you have made a huge

difference. Do the same."

I don't say another word. I pick up my mug and hold it out towards her.

"To us and our well-deserved successes," I say.

"To us and being awesome," she grins.

We click our cups together and drain the last dregs of the tea. It's not champagne, but it's a celebration, and we deserve it. I believe that I deserve it, I really do now.

The sound of a key in the front door snaps me back to the reality of life. I know it's Carl before he pushes into the house and stomps upstairs without so much as looking whether I am home. Zoe and I are still in the kitchen, tucked away at the back of the house, but he didn't call out, he didn't pop his head in. He doesn't care.

Zoe matches the change in my expression with one of her own. Her smile melts into a look of tender sympathy.

"I should…" I start to say.

She shrugs slightly. "You don't have to go running," she says. "Maybe it's better if you don't."

Maybe it is, but I can't stand the atmosphere of words left unsaid. I need to clear things up with Carl.

"Last night…" I say, and then I can't find any more words.

"Last night must have been horrible," she says. "Last night was last night. You don't want to go through that again, do you?"

"No."

Where has that confidence gone? I sound deflated, like the hope and happiness have been squeezed out of me. I settle back into my seat, trying to relax, but feeling the tension stiffening my body.

She lowers her voice. "I didn't want to get you talking about it. I thought we could just…you know…have some happy time."

"I know," I say. "Thank you."

My voice is as hushed as hers. I know how sound carries in this house, even with two floors between us and Carl.

"But it is what it is," she says. "Tell me what's going on. What did he say? What did he do?"

My sigh is long and draining.

"You know what you saw. If you want answers, you demand answers. You deserve the truth," she says.

"Do you think he would really do that?

What do you think?" I ask.

She breaks eye contact for a moment and appears to consider the answer.

"I don't know what to say, Vi. I only see things from the outside."

"That doesn't help much," I say. My voice is coarse, and I don't mean to sound so ungrateful. "Sorry," I add. "I…"

Before I finish the sentence, I hear the thudding of footsteps coming back downstairs. I instinctively put my finger to my lips and make a shushing sound. Zoe sits silently beside me as we listen to Carl's descent.

He walks into the kitchen, and without looking at Zoe, he addresses me.

"When you girls have quite finished talking about me, do you think you could have the decency to talk to me instead, Violet?"

I choke up, wordless, and nod timidly.

You girls. That's the exact term that Dad used to say when he would flip out at Mum and me. It's not completely out of context here.

"Actually…" Zoe begins to speak.

"Actually nothing. I wasn't talking to

you."

He throws the words at her, and for a split second I read surprise on her face. She soon recovers her composition though, and replies.

"Actually, we were talking about Violet. Not that it's any of your business what we talk about."

She may have told me that she didn't want to pass judgment, but Carl's tone isn't helping to show him in a positive light. I don't want the two of them to start an argument though I couldn't bear to be in the middle of that.

You girls. It's too close to the bone.

Chapter Twenty-Two

By the end of the week, Carl and I have barely spoken to each other. If there was a chance to save what we had, I missed it. From the moment I brought up the messages it has seemed like there's no going back. Carl is distant and defensive, and there's no talking to him.

I've tried.

I've really tried.

I want to believe him, and I want to trust him, but all that has happened is that he has become increasingly detached.

I don't know what I can do. All I know is that I have to do something.

He's been up in his room since he came back from uni today, and when he comes down, although I don't want him to think I'm ambushing him in any way, I walk nonchalantly behind him into the kitchen.

"Can we talk?" I say it as calmly as I can. I don't want him to think I'm about to make a scene.

"There's not much to talk about," he says.

"So, is this it? Is it over between us?"

I don't know what response I expected,

but I thought perhaps, just maybe, a part of him might want to work through this.

"Over?" he says. "Yes, it's over."

He turns his back, reaching up into the cupboard for his mug. His hand brushes past the mug that I usually use, but he only picks out his own.

"Can we, I mean is there…" I should have thought about what I was going to say, because now I am standing in the kitchen, close to tears, mumbling towards his back, and it doesn't feel great.

He spins dramatically and faces me.

"What? What are you trying to say? Come on, get it out."

"Why are you being like this? What changed? Why are…just, why?" I don't want to cry. Not now. Not in front of him. I never thought he could be like this. Last year he was such a good friend, so solid and supportive. Then he was a great boyfriend. Now? Now I barely recognise him.

"Nothing changed. Maybe that's the problem," he says.

I don't understand what he is saying, and it must show on my face.

"I can't handle this," he says. "I'm going

to move out."

"What? Where would you go? You don't have to…"

"I can hardly stay here with you and your friend who clearly hates me."

"She doesn't…I mean she sticks up for me, that's all."

"That's all? The pair of you are impossible. There's no room in your life for a relationship with your course and your friend, and your ridiculous paranoia. I thought you were done with that stupid anxiety."

I thought I was too.

"It's not stupid. I can't help it. Don't you think I've tried to…"

"You've tried nothing. You said you were going to get some help, and what happened there? You never bothered. You just hide behind it, use it as an excuse for everything in your stupid life. That's what hasn't changed. You haven't changed."

"My life isn't stupid either," I say, but my words don't sound certain.

"I felt sorry for you, okay? Last year when Luke and Zoe were all loved up and you were rattling around the house on your own, obsessing about these panic attacks or whatever they are. I felt sorry for you. I stopped seeing my mates so I could spend time with you, and now that I want to actually do something other than be stuck here with you all the time, it's a crime. You're unbelievable."

There are so many things I want to pick apart from that diatribe, but all I say is, "Doing something and doing someone are two different things."

I regret it the moment the words tumble from my mouth. Maybe I am stupid after all.

He glares at me and shakes his head slowly.

"What's the point?" he says. "I'm moving out. This is over. Whatever this is. It's over."

I know it's not what I should say, but my instinct is taking over my brain. "Did you ever actually like me?" I ask.

He looks at me, his face expressionless.

"Did you?" I ask again.

I want to shut up, I really do, but my heart is thudding so hard in my chest. I can't think clearly. I'm not saying or doing anything right. Perhaps I never do.

Without replying, he walks to the door,

moving within inches of me but not touching.

"Carl!"

He doesn't turn around.

He doesn't stop.

He doesn't answer the question.

Instead, he leaves me standing alone in the kitchen, and I finally let the tears flow.

Although I can barely concentrate on anything, I spend the rest of the evening working on my research project. The final assignment is a six-thousand-word literature review and discussion on my chosen topic. Maternal mental health in the antenatal period; I thought that was a great idea. When I started work on the project, I thought that I would focus on anxiety, but I found so much information on so many other mental health issues that I had to read more.

Learning about how best to support women has also given me some strategies for supporting myself. At the back of my mind, or perhaps not quite as far as the back, I must have known that this would happen. I didn't get the support from my GP or the counselling service that I very nearly accessed last year, but now, at the end of my three years, I feel more confident and in control than I ever have before. At least I did. I thought I did.

I have grown, not only grown older, although now I am in my early twenties rather than being the teenager that I was when I started my course. I have grown in confidence. I have grown in terms of my knowledge and skills, but isn't that the whole point of coming to university? No. Not the whole point. What I have learnt in the classroom and on the wards has been so much more than the contents of a book, or the slides from my lectures. I've learnt from the experience of the midwives that I have worked alongside, and the lecturers that have coached and mentored me through the theory. I've learnt from Zoe

I've learnt from my relationship with Carl, or at least I hope that I have. I don't want to think about him right now. I don't want what happened, what is still happening, between he and I, the way he has behaved, the way he's making me feel, any of it, I don't want that to cast a shadow over my experience. I don't want it to cloud my happiness. Passing my course, learning the life lessons along the way, that is my achievement, and I am going to celebrate it.

I know he is in the house, in Tangiers Court, the place that Zoe and I found and made our home. He's just upstairs. I could go and try to talk to him, to say something, anything to try to put things right, but I know that it's too late. It's too late because he has let me down. This isn't my doing. I haven't failed, I have been failed.

Did he actually ever like me? He didn't reply, and I can't let myself become obsessed with what the answer, the true answer, would be. What I do need to do is to like myself. At the moment I feel fragile and my heart is heavy with loss, but a part of me, the stronger part, knows that I can learn from this and move on as a stronger person.

Eventually.

Chapter Twenty-Three

The week before Easter break, as I'm coming towards the end of my antenatal placement, Carl moves out. I'm surprised that he has stayed as long as this; the past five weeks have been unimaginably uncomfortable. We have tried to avoid each other in the house, but the atmosphere has been a thick fog of awkwardness.

When Zoe, Luke, and I have been downstairs, watching television, Carl has kept himself hidden away up in his room. It's almost felt like the beginning of last year when we barely saw him or spoke to him. When I barely knew him.

It's wrong to think of it like this, but if Zoe and Luke weren't together perhaps Carl and I would never had become a couple either. We drifted into the relationship at a time that I was vulnerable and weak; I'm not saying that he took advantage of that, not at all but perhaps if I had been spending more time with Zoe I wouldn't have felt the need to fill my time with something (someone) else.

Up until Carl, Zoe had been my only

confidante, my only true friend. I thought I had been lucky enough to find a boyfriend who would fill that role too, but I was wrong.

While I'm on my antenatal placement, I realise that Zoe isn't the only person I have to talk to. I've drawn the Sunday afternoon shift with my mentor, Becky, this week, and there are only three women staying with us right now.

The busiest time for antenatal ward tends to be weekdays. Women are referred in by their GPs or community midwives, and there are fewer opportunities for referrals at the weekend. Most of our intake on Saturday and Sunday tends to come from delivery suite. Women who attend for blood pressure checks that aren't in need of constant one-on-one care, or those whose waters have broken but they aren't in labour yet; there are many reasons why women might stay on the antenatal ward, but today there's a lull, and I'm appreciative.

I should want it to be busy. Being busy means there is more opportunity to learn. The more I see, the more I experience, the more I can reflect on. Right now, I am finding it difficult to focus, and it must show.

We've done the drugs round, which took us all of ten minutes, and we're settling back in the office with tea and a box of chocolates that one of last week's patients left for us. There's a copy of *What's New?* magazine, a trashy gossip mag that I would never dream of buying, but that seems to be the staple read of people who are stuck in a hospital ward with not a lot to do. I'm about to reach over for it, when Becky speaks.

"You seem a bit distant today," she says.

It takes me aback. My first thought leaps towards whether I have been acting unprofessionally, or not engaging with the patients fully. Whatever is going on in my life, I must put their needs first. When I am here, I am Violet Cobham, Student Midwife. Violet the Heartbroken Idiot has to stay at home.

"Sorry," I say.

Becky picks up on my surprise and shakes her head. "You haven't done anything wrong. You're not your usual self though. I've hardly seen you smile all day."

I have a choice. I can throw back a joke,

try to deflect from what is bothering me, or I can open up and chat to Becky about how I am feeling.

I don't know her particularly well. I've had three placements on this ward, and she has been my mentor for each. Not that we have worked every shift together, there have been times when she hasn't been around when I have been on duty, and of course I usually try to avoid late shifts on Mondays. Still, we have talked.

It was Becky that encouraged me to visit the mother and baby mental health centre at the Linden Unit last year. Without her prompting me, I would have missed out on so much. Although we have never talked about it again, she told me then, when she was suggesting that I visit the unit as one of my SPOKE optional placement days, that she had suffered with mental health issues. She might actually understand how I feel.

"I'm…" I start the sentence before I have even decided what I want to say. How much do I want to tell her? I take a breath, try to calm my heart rate, and speak again. "I'm not sleeping well. The anxiety is, well, it's pretty bad at the moment. I split up with my boyfriend, or at least he split up with me, which is the same thing, of course, but you know what I mean, and, well, I feel rubbish."

It's not the most concise of explanations, and I stumble over the phrasing, but I get the words out.

"Oh Vi. I'm sorry to hear that. Do you want to talk about it?"

Do I? I haven't even told Zoe about the way that my anxiety has been bubbling away since Carl dumped me. My sleep pattern is all over the place, I can't concentrate on anything anymore. I don't want to worry her. We both have to study; we both need to focus. I don't want to monopolise her attention, not now.

"I feel so stupid," I say. "Inadequate. Like I wasn't good enough for him. I feel like if I was more interesting, or at least less boring, he wouldn't have left me. There's something wrong with me."

I can't make eye contact. Even though I never made it to see a counsellor, I imagine that this is what it might be like. Becky has been a midwife for a while, and I'm sure she must have counselled plenty of patients. Probably not quite as many daft students

207

though.

"You can't think like that," she says calmly. "If he left you, for whatever reason, it doesn't mean that it was your fault."

"I think there was someone else. I found a message. He never said there was, he never admitted to it, but everything fell apart after I confronted him."

"You read his messages?" she asks.

Her voice doesn't contain any traces of judgment, it sounds more like she is trying to clarify what happened.

"No," I say. "Well, yes. One message. It was on his phone screen. I didn't mean to, and I couldn't unsee it."

"It is pretty difficult to unsee things," Becky smiles. "Was everything alright until then?"

I nod, and then I reconsider. "Maybe not, no. I felt like something was off, but I didn't know what it was."

"Sounds like you've had a tough time of it. I can see why you're feeling down. I know from my own experience how easy it is to take things to heart and blame yourself for everything that goes wrong."

I can feel a lump growing in my throat.

I'm worried that I'm going to burst into tears, right here in the office. My back is to the door, at least no one would see me if they walked past, but this isn't right. I shouldn't be doing this, not here.

"I shouldn't have said anything," I sigh.

"My role as your mentor is to support you," Becky says, leaning forward and placing her hand on my knee. "We have time to talk, and if that makes you feel any better at all, let's do it. Okay?"

"I was fine before I met him. Not fine. I mean I had the anxiety, but I didn't need a boyfriend. I didn't need this. I didn't want to fall in love and be let down and feel like –"

"Like rubbish," Becky nods. "No one should be able to make you feel that way. What would you say if it was one of your friends that this had happened to, and they were telling you about it?"

Zoe. What would I tell Zoe if she were moping around, losing sleep over some guy that clearly doesn't deserve her?

It's not that simple. Anxiety doesn't stop grabbing hold of you and shaking you just because you tell it that you want it to leave you alone. Once it gets hold it sinks its claws in and hangs on for dear life. I want to say that I would tell her she'd better off without him, and that she should forget him and move on, but I know that isn't going to make me feel better. There's no instant miracle cure.

"I'd tell her to be good to herself," I say.

Becky drinks her tea and appears to toss my words over.

"That's a good start," she says. "Be good to yourself."

As she finishes repeating my advice back to me a buzzer rings down the ward. I instinctively start to stand up and respond. Instead, Becky taps my leg again.

"I'll get it," she says. "Take a minute, okay?"

I nod silently and let her go.

Being good to myself has never been easy. Anxiety causes me to be unnecessarily hard on myself, but I never know at the time quite how unnecessary it is. Just like Carl, it makes me believe that I am useless, of no value. Being good to myself means fighting against that, giving myself a break, and a chance to move forward.

It's what I need to do, I know. There are

more important things in my life than
worrying about a man who was *not* good to
me.

Chapter Twenty-Four

Little by little I try to make a change. When I lie awake in bed at night, worrying about why he left me, wondering what is so wrong with me, I try to distract myself and push the thoughts away.

The break-up still stings, but I am trying to look for the positives. That's the only way that I can deal with this.

I've tried not to obsess over the details. I have to accept that there are some questions that are going to remain unanswered. Did I do something wrong? How long had it been going on? Who was she? Why? That, most of all: why? It's unknowable.

Instead of letting my over-anxious, self-doubting brain take over and punish me for whatever it is that I did or didn't do, I am trying to focus on my research project. I'm meant to hand it in after the final block in uni, before our last placements. They like us to be able to focus on wrapping up the PADs and concentrating on our clinical allocations, but that means I only have just over a month to finish my assignment. That may sound easy, but I've gathered so much information that trying to work out what to include and what to leave out is a major task on its own.

The house is quiet, with Luke asleep on the sofa downstairs and Zoe across the landing in her room, working on her own dissertation. Sure, we could take our laptops and sit next to each other at the kitchen table, but we would soon turn away from the walls of text on the screens and start to chat about much more interesting things. Being supportive sometimes means being apart. Knowing that she is knuckling down to her work makes me more determined to get stuck into mine.

I'm getting there, slowly. The bulk of my paper is about anxiety in pregnancy, and I have written up most of what I have researched. I click onto a tab to open a search engine, and momentarily I'm distracted by one of my social media accounts. It's not because I see something that I have to read; I've not received any notifications, and it's not a funny cat video that pops up and takes my attention away from my assignment. I wish that it were. I would have much preferred that. Instead, I

213

have a thought that stops me in my tracks. I forget what I was about to search for, and I stare blankly at the screen.

Carl.

I'm thinking about Carl.

Specifically I'm thinking back to the day that turned out to be the beginning of the end: when I confronted him about the message.

The first thing he looked at when he opened my phone was my social media. That was where he expected to find some kind of sign that I had been up to no good. To be fair, I don't think he really expected to find anything. Anybody that knows me would be able to confirm that I am at my happiest at home with close friends and family. Having one relationship is hard enough for me, never mind two-timing anyone. I barely use social media, compared to a lot of girls my age, and even if someone tried to send me untoward messages I probably wouldn't see them.

But Carl went straight to my inbox.

I should be closing this browser page and getting on with my database search, I know, but now that I have the thought in my head, I can't get away from it. Morbid curiosity is driving me to dig deeper. I bring up his profile and read his *'About Me'* details. His name, date of birth, hometown, are all listed. His relationship status is set to single. He either changed that back quickly or he never updated it at all. I don't care, it doesn't matter, but it does make me pause for a moment.

I can see his friends list, so I scroll through, looking for a girl whose name begins with **B**. He has over a thousand friends. I, on the other hand, have eighty. I have friends from high school, family members, uni students, and some of the midwives. Everyone on my list is someone that I actually know and want to keep in touch with. I don't think he has actually met Lauren Jade from Alabama, but I could be wrong. Most of the people on his list are indeed girls and young women. There are a couple of lads from his course, whose names I vaguely recognise him saying, and some based in Leicester, so I assume they are friends from home, but the majority of pictures show perfectly posed pretty selfies.

"What were you ever doing with me?" I ask myself the question out loud, and it hangs heavily in the air.

This isn't evidence of anything. Without trying to hack into his account, which I have no intention of doing, and I wouldn't even if I had the first idea how to, all I can say is that Carl knows lots of attractive girls. There's no rules against that.

I can't scroll through the full list of friends, and I have no idea how to search for B amongst the many names. This is hopeless. All I am doing is making myself feel bad, and it's stopping me from doing my work.

We had something, and now it's over.

Unfortunately, although I have failed to gain any new information about Carl, I have also failed to gain any new information for my assignment. My head is spinning, and I know I should never have let myself think about him, let alone creep through his social media. I click back onto his profile page and look at his most recent photo. He's a looker, that's for sure. How did I ever imagine that he would really be interested in me?

Forget it. I can't possibly concentrate on my essay now. I close my laptop and walk as quietly as I can across to my door. I am going to hate myself for doing this, but sometimes my emotions take over, and I can't reason with them. I step onto the landing and listen against Zoe's door. Her fingers are tapping away at the keyboard, so she is either on a roll with her essay, or she is playing around on the internet too. Either way, the sound of my footsteps hasn't disturbed her. I walk to the stairs, but instead of going down to the kitchen, which is probably, almost certainly, what I should do, I start to climb up.

I know he is gone. There is no trace of him here anymore. He took everything, threw away his rubbish, washed his bedding and wiped away any signs that he ever lived in this room. It's empty and cold, and seeing it like this hits home. I was barely even up here, but this room was his. I suck in a deep breath, trying to catch the scent of him, but there's nothing. Even that has been erased.

Before I can stop myself, tears are spilling from my eyes. So many questions. So much that no amount of research would ever be able to answer. I can find out how to help other people, but who is going to help me?

That question, it seems, does have an

answer.

"Hey," a voice comes from behind me.

Startled, I don't know whether to wipe my eyes or speak, and I whirl around without doing either.

"Oh no," Luke says. "Oh, Vi. Come here. It's okay."

And so I do. I step across the landing, into his outstretched arms. His hug feels safe and warm, and it's exactly what I need.

"You shouldn't do this to yourself." He says the words into my hair. "He didn't deserve you. I know that is probably one of the biggest clichés in the book, but that doesn't stop it being true."

I reach up awkwardly and try to wipe my eyes so that my mascara doesn't end up on his T-shirt.

"I feel so stupid," I say.

"It wasn't your fault. Whatever happened wasn't your fault."

More clichés, and this time I definitely can't agree.

"I feel stupid for feeling like this now. I feel stupid for missing him when he treated me like an idiot."

"You are a lot of things, Violet, but you

are not an idiot. My wonderful girlfriend would not have an idiot for a best friend, that's for certain."

I make a tiny sad laughing noise that makes me sound like a piglet. With Luke though, I don't care.

Zoe's footsteps sound their way up the stairs, and she joins us on the cramped upper landing.

"No one invited me to the party," she smiles, and wraps her arms around both of us, creating a group hug.

"Violet was making herself feel sad," Luke says.

"Anything to get out of studying," Violet says, and I can hear the smile in her voice.

"A girl has to work hard to get a hug around here." I sniff back my tears and relax into the hug.

The door to Carl's room is behind me. All I can see is Luke's T-shirt. All I can feel is their arms embracing me. With them on my side, I can get through this.

I have to get through it.

However bad I feel about what has happened with Carl, and however confused I am about why, I can't let it take over my thoughts. Although I have made it through my OSCE, which is by far the most daunting of my assessments this year, I still have assignments to hand in, my research project to complete and, of course, always hanging over me, the rest of my PAD to get signed off.

I'm tumbling towards my final term, and that in itself is enough to make me feel the pressure.

Chapter Twenty-Five

Compared to the emotional turmoil of going home for Christmas without Carl, being able to spend Easter with my mum with no fear of divided loyalties is actually a relief.

Once Easter break is over, I have a final four weeks in uni before I am due out onto placements. I want to be on the ward, getting the last of my paperwork signed off.

Being in uni feels like a waste of time now. There's only my research paper to hand in. The lectures are focussed on the transition from student to qualified midwife, what to expect from our preceptorship periods and, perhaps most immediately important, advice on how to approach our job interviews.

We are lucky. There are going to be a handful of jobs available at all the local units. That doesn't necessarily mean that we will all get taken on at our first choice of hospital. It doesn't necessarily mean that we will be offered a job at all. There is still a procedure to be followed, and we have to impress the Head of Midwifery and whoever else interviews us.

Interviews fill me with dread; all the

attention focussed upon me, with so much opportunity to make a mess of things is almost unbearable. My whole future will be riding on how I perform, what I say, and what they think of me. I can only hope that the second interviewer is someone that knows me. Not only because they might forgive me more easily if I slip up, but also because knowing someone will make me feel more relaxed. A little bit more, anyway.

I've already filled in my application for St. Jude's before I start back on my placement. It finally strikes me that my delivery suite mentor bears almost the same name as the hospital that we work in. Jade. Jude. It's close. I can't help but take it as a positive omen. Not that I necessarily believe in that kind of thing, but anything that helps me to feel more positive and less terrified has to be a bonus. Either that or I am stretching it, trying to clutch at anything to give me some hope. I am stretching it. I'm stretching it really thinly, I know.

At the beginning of my placement I have six deliveries left to have signed off. Every time I open up my PAD those empty spaces still mock me. This has hung over me all year. I don't want to wish away the end of my course, but I want to have everything done and dusted, signed and sealed, and yes, very much delivered.

By the last week of my placement I have one more delivery to tick off on my PAD checklist. I've conducted all of the postnatal, antenatal and neonatal checks that I needed to; those sheets are filled with signatures and ready to be submitted. I've written statements and reflections.

This is it. This is my last week, and all I need to do is support one more woman to deliver her baby. I have to see one more life into the world. That's not hard work, it's a privilege, but the pressure of needing this one thing so that I can complete my PAD and submit it feels intense.

If I don't manage to deliver a baby this week I'll need to stay on for more shifts after I'm meant to have finished. That's the worst-case scenario. I have all week to do this. I have longer if I need it. I can do it. I will do it. It's fine.

I repeat that over in my head as I walk

into the hospital and up to delivery suite.
Still I feel the tension of anxiety fluttering
through every inch of my body.

"It's fine, it's fine," I repeat to myself,
this time out loud, softly, beneath my breath.
"It's fine."

As I get to the double doors of the unit I
pause, take a deep inhalation, and try to
compose myself.

The ward is eerily, disappointingly quiet.
There's a distinct atmosphere when it's busy,
even without the noise from the rooms, the
air feels somehow charged. Today, it is calm
and peaceful. By the time I get to the
midwives' office I have already resigned
myself to an uneventful day.

Jade nods at the board, as blank as I
expected it to be, and says, "Sorry."

"Oh gosh, it's hardly your fault," I smile,
despite my disappointment. "I have all week,
really it's okay."

"And if it doesn't happen this week, you
can stay on," she winks.

I know she is being playful, but I really
don't even want to think about that. I have
all week; I'm sure something will happen.

"You should have been here yesterday,"

one of the other midwives says. "Board full of women. There was a second-year student here, got three deliveries. Shell, it was. Do you know her?"

Shell, the name sounds familiar. Well, good for her. Perhaps she won't have the last-minute panic that I am having.

"If you'd called me I would have come in," I say.

I'm joking, but it strikes me that if someone had called, I would have been here, regardless of it not being my planned placement day. Maybe that's what it will come to; I'll put myself on call. I can't miss then.

I'm tossing the thought over in my head when Sister speaks. "Someone did phone up earlier. First-time mum, having niggles. Didn't sound like much was happening, but you never know."

"You never know," I agree.

"Have you got anything else that needs to be signed off?" Jade asks.

I pull my PAD out from my bag, and flick through, showing her the relevant pages.

"Just my end of course meeting with you and the placement mentor, Deb, and this."

The list of names, all in my trying-to-be-neat handwriting, of the women whose babies I have delivered during my course. Even with the gaping hole at the bottom where the final sign-off will go, it feels like a huge achievement. I remember every single one of those women, their babies, and my experience of supporting them. I hope it will always be this way; I never want to forget anyone. I hope it will never become just a job.

"I know," Jade says, reading my expression. "All those women," she smiles.

She has been beside me, or behind me, for nearly every delivery. We have worked together through most of my time on the ward.

"Thank you," I say. It comes from nowhere, and it feels so insufficient. "Really, thank you. You've been great."

She shrugs and smiles again.

"When you have qualified, you'll have the privilege of mentoring students too. Don't forget how you feel right now, at this present moment. The excitement, the trepidation. Hold onto it."

I nod. I won't forget. I'm sure I won't.

Chapter Twenty-Six

We chat for what seems like an hour until we're interrupted by the ringing of the ward phone. It's an outside call, I've learned how to tell the difference.

Sister picks up and talks to the person on the other end of the line. By the time the call ends, I know that we are getting a visitor. I look at the ward sister expectantly for the details.

"Yes, it's a lady for you," she says. "Not the one who phoned up before, someone different. Second baby, thirty-nine weeks, sounds like she's in labour. Here." She holds out a scrap of paper with the woman's hospital number so that I can pull the notes from the file.

"Anything else we need to know?" I ask. I want to make sure I get everything ready and get everything right.

"Nope," says Sister. "Routine pregnancy. Waters haven't broken yet. Last time everything was normal." She shrugs. "Get the notes and have a read while she's on the way."

Nodding, I glance quickly at Jade and

then set off for the clinic where the records are kept. All the way there, all the time I am browsing for the notes, and all the way back the only thing I can think about is how this could be it. My final delivery.

My patient today is Hester Healey, and as Sister rightly said, there is nothing remarkable in her notes. The main hospital file has all of her medical history, as well as her obstetric records. She's been to clinic for a routine visit, but most of her care has been out in the community. The only other notes in her file are from an appendectomy some years ago, which won't have any bearing on her delivery. Routine. Normal.

When I return to delivery suite, I manage to fill a jug with water for Hester and take it to her room before she arrives. She's a petite brunette, and accompanying her is her rather tall husband, Jeff.

I introduce myself, take a history, and pop back into the office to talk to Jade.

"Everything okay?" she asks.

"Seems fine," I say. "The contractions are getting stronger and lasting longer. She doesn't want any pain relief yet."

Jade nods. "I think you can take the lead on this one. You know I have to be there for the delivery, but everything else, unless you need me, you should go it alone."

I instinctively look over to the ward sister, and she also nods in confirmation.

"You'll be fine," she says.

I did feel fine before I knew I was going to do this alone. Now, I feel more nervous than I ever have previously on my placements.

"You will," Jade says. "You basically do everything anyway, right?"

She has given me a lot of opportunity to lead and learn how to support women in my own way, that's true. But she has always been physically by my side too.

"Okay." I look her in the eyes. "Thanks. This will be good practice."

"Anything at all, ask."

With that, I go back into Hester's room.

Not having Jade with me makes me feel as though I am missing a limb. Of course, I have explained to Hester and Jeff that I am a final year student, about to qualify, and that Jade is only a few steps away.

"Must be lovely being a midwife," she says. "I couldn't do it myself, with all that blood and..." She screws her face up rather than finishing the sentence.

"There's not all that much," I smile.

"Have you always wanted to be a midwife?" she asks.

"Since as far back as I can remember," I say.

"I'm a project manager," she says. "That's not one of the jobs people dream of, but I love it."

"That's what matters," I smile.

Our chatter is broken by the onset of a contraction. Hester focuses on the tightening of her abdomen and the rising pain, breathing deeply throughout.

"That's it," Jeff coaches her. "Keep breathing like that."

Everything seems as straightforward as her first delivery, and as routine as the rest of her pregnancy has been. We carry on chatting between contractions, and it feels like we are building a bond. I love this part of midwifery. Even if I don't end up delivering the baby I know I will have had a great experience today.

I pop out to the office for my lunch, and Jade steps in to support Hester and Jeff, and to carry on with the check-ups. We carry on monitoring pulse, fetal heart rate, and contractions frequently, as well as keeping an eye on blood pressure and urine output. Her waters still haven't broken, and she hasn't had any bleeding, but we keep a check on any vaginal loss too.

I've been on my feet for hours, but it doesn't feel like it, and as soon as I sit to eat my sandwich, I wish I were back in the room. I don't want to miss anything.

Typically, I'm about three bites in when Jade comes back into the office.

"She's getting the urge to push now, Vi. I don't think she'll be long."

I look at the bread in my hand, and then back at Jade.

"You'll probably be okay to finish that. Don't give yourself indigestion. I'll set up a trolley."

"Thanks, Jade."

I try to take my time over the rest of my lunch, but all I can think about is getting back into the room and getting my head back into the situation. I gulp down the rest of the food, swill it down with my tea, wash my hands and get back to work.

Jade has just finished setting up the trolley, and she's standing up by Hester's top half, stroking her hair and speaking softly.

"Everything's set. I don't think you need to do an examination; I can see some movement down there during contractions now."

"Okay," I agree. "Let's see what happens then. Alright, Hester?"

Hester gives a quiet grunt of acceptance.

"Is that urge to push getting stronger?" I ask.

She nods.

"Try to have a quick drink before your next contraction," I suggest.

Jeff leans over, from the opposite side to Jade, and hands her the little cup of water. "That's it."

I've learned all of the things I should say and do. There's so much to remember. I have to make sure that I am thinking of Hester's comfort as well as monitoring what is happening with the labour. This is as much about making her experience as positive as possible as it is delivering her baby.

She thrusts the cup back at her husband as the next contraction starts to build.

"Well done," I say. "I'm going to have a look down below, see if I can see anything, okay?"

Hester is trying to focus on the breathing, just as she did before, but as the contraction gets stronger, her body gives a forceful push.

Jade was right. I can see the top of baby's head move towards me as Hester pushes. It's a little dark circle, up in the distance, but I recognise it for what it is. With each push I see a little more of the circle.

"Brilliant," I say. "Baby is moving."

I reach up and press the heart rate monitor onto Hester's abdomen, making sure there's still a strong, steady heartbeat, and that it isn't slowing with the contraction. It sounds perfect. I take the opportunity to look at Jade, and she nods supportively.

The contractions come every couple of minutes. Sometimes, with some women, contractions can space out at this point, but Hester's remain strong and regular. Each time she pushes I see her baby move closer towards me down the birth canal. Pushing is sometimes a two-steps-forward-one-step-back process until the baby passes around the natural curve of the pelvis. When it gets to the point that baby's head doesn't slide back anymore between contractions, I know she is nearly there.

"Shouldn't be long now," I tell her. "You're doing so well."

Hester tries to smile. Her face is sweat-lined and she's resting her head against her husband between contractions. Jade has hold of a damp cloth that she has been wiping Hester's face with to cool her down.

"Nearly there," Jade says.

"Okay, love. Nearly there," Jeff repeats.

It takes two more contractions for the head to crown. Hester pants when I ask her to pant, and baby's head is born. Looping my finger around, below baby's head, looking for any sign of the cord being wrapped around there is an instinctive move to me now. I notice though as I'm doing this that the baby has remarkably chubby cheeks and the head is bigger than I have seen before.

A strange sick feeling hits my gut, and I look over to Jade, trying to appear as calm as possible.

"It's a big baby," I say.

When I palpated Hester's abdomen, the baby didn't feel particularly large. I don't think I missed anything. There's nothing in the notes to say that any of the other midwives who have assessed her suspected that this could be a big baby. Even Jade, who has been in here and cared for Hester on my break, didn't think anything untoward.

But this is a big baby, and a big baby plus a not-so-tall woman can lead to shoulder dystocia. I may have passed my OSCE and be trained to deal with an emergency situation, but I don't want it to actually happen. My usual calm and controlled exterior is starting to crack. I can't let it show.

"How much did your first baby weigh?" I ask.

"Seven and a half pounds," Jeff answers. "Is this lad going to be bigger?"

"We're about to find out," I say.

Jade is beside the emergency buzzer; she knows the drill too.

As the next contraction rises, I say, "Push now, Hester. As hard as you can."

I guide the head, tying to move the anterior shoulder under the pubic arch. My

235

heart is thudding out of my chest. It's too hot in this room. Everything suddenly feels too close, too much for me to deal with.

It moves. The shoulder moves. It seems like minutes rather than the seconds it actually takes. The baby slides out of the birth canal; a healthy, chubby boy, just as Jeff said.

"He's fine." I take a deep breath of relief.

"Well done," Jade says, and I know she is talking to me, just as much as to Hester.

My mind was running through the mnemonic, thinking about what I would need to do if the shoulder hadn't delivered, and also second guessing whether I should have picked up on something sooner.

When we get back into the office, Jade speaks to me.

"Well spotted," she says. "Nine pounds, spot on. Quite a bit bigger than her last."

"I missed it though."

"Me too," she says. "And everyone else that's been looking after her. But when you saw it, you knew. That's the first step."

As we drink tea and fill in the notes we talk about what we would have done and

236

what we could have done. Reflecting on practice, on individual cases as well as on our general experiences is an important part of training and will carry on being important when I am working as a qualified midwife. It's a constant learning process, and I will never know everything there is to know. What I do know is that there is always someone to talk to, always someone to share my thoughts with, and always someone to support me.

I finish typing the records into the computer database and sink back into my chair. It's been an unexpectedly draining day. The clock shows ten minutes left until the end of shift, and I want to take Hester and her baby up to the ward myself and handover before I leave.

"Thanks for today," I say to Jade.

"No problem. You did great."

I smile and get up to go back to Hester's room.

"Are you forgetting something?" Jade asks.

I stand and think, and nothing comes.

Jade points at my PAD folder, sticking out of the top of my bag.

I can get my final delivery signed off. I did almost forget, even though that seems unimaginable. I was caught up in the experience and focussing on the task at hand. My sign-off sheet became the furthest thing from my mind. As I always hoped, it has been about the experience, and about supporting women, rather than about ticking off the numbers. That said, I can relax and enjoy the remaining days of my placement now, without having to worry about how many babies I do or don't deliver.

I hand my file to Jade, and she signs her name at the bottom of the list, below all her other signatures.

All I can do is smile proudly and thank her again. For everything.

Chapter Twenty-Seven

The rest of the week feels a lot more relaxed, now that I'm not chasing deliveries to fill in my PAD. I actually make it to supporting forty-four women in delivering their babies by the end of my final shift on Saturday morning. Then that's it. My last day on placement. My final day as a student midwife. It's surreal.

My last day on placement is also the last time that I will see a lot of my course mates. We've arranged a get-together in the union bar to celebrate the end of the three years. Even with my dislike of the bar, I am too emotional to worry about that today. My brain doesn't know whether to be happy or sad, excited about what I have achieved or afraid of what might happen in the future. I'm all over the place, but I have made it.

By eight o'clock, I'm in the union bar drinking diet cola, and I don't even feel like I'm missing out. Sure, I've tried to have a few drinks when I've been out here before, but it never ends well for me. I don't enjoy the way alcohol affects my anxiety, so I have finally made the sensible decision not to drink. It actually feels like quite a weight has been lifted. Even though I am still not particularly comfortable in such a large crowd, at least I am doing it on my own terms now, and making my own choices.

That feels good.

Tonight is a chance to say goodbye to Ashley, Sophie, and the other girls from my course. I'll be seeing Simon on the wards if we both get the jobs that we have applied for, so it's a *see you soon* rather than *'goodbye'* to him. I'll keep in touch with Ash and Soph though. I can't wait to hear what their new hospitals are like, and what experiences they have in their careers. We are on our own, but we are together. We are a community.

Zoe and Luke have come out with me, and somehow Luke has persuaded Zoe to join him and his course mates, Rajesh, Flo, and Damon, around the pool table. I've never seen her play before, and I've chosen to stay at the table and save our seats rather than join in. It's a reasonable excuse. I really couldn't bear to make a complete idiot of myself trying to take part in a game I have absolutely no clue how to play.

I'm going to sit here for ten minutes, soak in the atmosphere without having to stumble through the crowd, and drink my non-alcoholic drink. This is the last time I will be here. I'm going to try to enjoy it.

And then I see him.

Not only do I see him, but he's seen me first, and he's walking in my direction.

Carl. Of course, Carl.

He looks different, somehow, but in many ways still the same. The same man I fell in love with. The same man who dumped me.

I should be over it by now. Seeing him walk towards me shouldn't make me feel physically sick, but it does.

"Violet," he says.

His voice slurs enough to let me know that he's had more than a couple of drinks. Would he have come to talk to me otherwise? He's got a glass with him, sloshing around a measure of something that looks like it's probably whiskey. I never knew he drank that; I never really knew him at all.

"Carl," I reply.

My eyes dart around the room, looking

for Zoe and Luke, hoping that they are heading back to the table. Of course, they aren't. I can't see the foyer or the pool table from here, but I know they haven't been gone long enough to be due back just yet. How long does pool take? I don't know how much time I can bear spending with Carl.

He slouches into the empty chair beside me and leans in towards me. The alcohol that has no doubt made him feel the need to come and talk to me hangs heavy on his breath.

"So good to see you," he says, in a mock-posh accent. It doesn't suit him.

I want to give him a snarky response. My instinct is to lash out and say that is it most definitely not good to see him, but that's not the kind of person I am.

"How's things?" I ask, instead.

"Everything is peachy," he says. "Just peachy. Looking forward to getting out of this place and going home."

For a moment I think he means the bar, but it strikes me that he's probably referring to the end of uni and moving home to Leicester. This thought comes with a strange feeling of relief. If he goes back there I won't ever run into him again.

"That's…good," I say.

I'm trying to pick my words carefully. I don't want a conversation, let alone an argument.

"You're looking…" He pauses, letting his eyes appraise me in a way that makes me feel even more uncomfortable. "…the same."

"Well, thanks," I say, not rising to the bait.

I'm not going to start an argument with him. Not here, not now, not ever.

"I wanted to say so-"

"Don't," I say, cutting him off. "I don't want to hear that you're sorry."

He laughs. He actually laughs. It's an ugly, twisted laugh, and I wish, wish, wish that he would disappear.

"I wanted to say something," he says, his voice trying to steady itself. "I thought I should come over and…" He waves his hand in front of his face like he's batting away smoke, and says, "…clear the air."

"Well, yes. It's very clear now, thank you," I say.

I haven't a clue what I am supposed to say. I thought I would never see him again. There was a time that I wanted to see him, that I thought that seeing him might be a good thing. This is not a good thing. Not at all.

He laughs again, and I don't feel any of the trademark sensations of anxiety. I feel anger. I look him dead in the eye and I ask the question that I have wanted to ask ever since we split up.

"For my own peace of mind, tell me. Were you seeing someone else?"

My voice remains calm and steady. I don't let my emotion spill out, even though it's trying to.

"That's how you get your peace of mind is it? Have you been torturing yourself all this time? Let it go. Move on. We're young, Violet. We should be having fun. You should be having fun."

He raises his glass to me.

"Get a drink. Get a few. Live a little."

I keep a hold of my emotions. I have to stay calm. I have to stay in control of myself.

"Thanks," I say. "You know I don't really drink."

"You don't really do anything. That's the problem."

I don't rise to it. I look him dead in the

eye and say, "It's not a problem for me. I love what I do. I love who I am. I'm sorry you felt differently."

That seems to slow him in his tracks. I think he's going to give up, turn away and walk off, but as he starts to move he stops again.

I'm not prepared for what comes next.

"Do you know why I was with you?"

"What?" The question seems to come from nowhere.

"Do you know why I was with you?" he uses exactly the same words and the same tone.

What kind of a question is that? We got on well. We were friends. He was lovely, back then, back when we spent our time chatting and laughing. I don't know how to answer, so I stand, silent, wishing he would go away or that I had the sense to walk off rather than listen to this.

"I'll tell you why." His face is right up close to mine now. His breath is heavy with lager and whiskey and something else that I can't even recognise. "You were vulnerable. That's why. I started giving you some attention. I knew that you would lap it up.

You were…well, you were so focussed on poor little Violet. Poor me, my friend has got a boyfriend and I'm all on my own now. Poor me, I can't do my exams because I'm too scared. Poor me —"

"You can stop right there." It's Zoe. She's standing beside him, and although I know she would never physically accost anyone, I can see the rage bristling through her.

I raise my hand to stop her. "Zoe, it's fine," I say.

I turn my attention to Carl. "You dated me because I was vulnerable, and because it was easy for you. I think that says a lot more about you than it does about me. Are you happy? Are you really happy now? You don't look it. But I tell you what, Carl. I am. I'm happy. I have everything that I could possibly want. I passed those exams. I finished my course. And yes, I have my best friend, and I love her. I don't care what you say, or what anyone says."

Instead of biting back he looks at me, long and hard, and then looks at Zoe. He starts to clap, slowly.

"Well done, Violet," he says. "Well done. I thought you were going to be a little mouse all your life, but maybe there is more to you. Good. Good for you."

Perhaps a part of him means those words, but they sound hollow.

Zoe flashes her eyes at me, as if asking a question. I can feel it. I know she wants to know if I'm okay, and if she should say something. I give her a tiny shake of the head. I want to handle this myself.

"It was great to catch up with you," I say, and I try to make the words light and pleasant, even though they mean goodbye.

Taking the hint, Zoe settles into the seat to the other side of me. We turn to each other and start to chat. The two of us form a bubble that he is not a part of, and he sits on the outside, looking like he has no idea what to do. Although I am trying to look nonchalant, the adrenaline that is pumping through me is making me dizzy, and I can barely focus on the conversation.

"Well, I have to get back to Bella," he says, putting all of the emphasis on the first letter of her name. "She'll probably be thinking I've run away with someone." I can't help but look at him when he says it. "Right, Vi?"

Without another word, he stumbles to his feet, turns his back, and disappears into the crowd.

Chapter Twenty-Eight

My course has ended, my placements are over, and I've done everything I need to do to qualify. Handing in my dissertation and my PAD feels surreal, but it also feels like a huge weight has been lifted.

I can almost relax and enjoy a few weeks off before I start work. Almost. First, I must get through an interview and be offered a job.

During my course I've given presentations, stumbled through the three OSCEs and talked about myself and my progress at regular meetings with my placement supervisor and my mentors. I'm trying to see my interview as just another meeting, but I know it's not. I know that it means everything. If I mess up now, all the work that I have put in over the past three years will have been for nothing.

And yes, it's interview singular. I want to stay at St. Jude's hospital, so it's the only position that I have applied for. I tossed it over in my head for a long time, but I think I am making the right decision. I know that if I want the job, I must do my best. It's a way of focusing my mind. If it all goes horribly wrong, I could look around and see where else there are vacancies, but I want to stay here. I want to be near to Mum. I want to stay close to Zoe and Luke. This is my life, the life that I have been building, and I want it to be my future.

The night before my interview, Zoe, Luke, and I are sitting in the back yard at Tangiers Court. We've been out here so many times over the past three years. The fairy lights flicker along the trellis, Luke has fired up the chimenea that we picked up cheap on one of our Saturday shopping trips, and we've got our terribly boring diet colas on the white metal table that Zoe and I bought right at the start of our tenancy.

Three years. Has it really been that long?

"How are you feeling about tomorrow?" Luke asks.

He's got his chair pulled right up to Zoe's so that he can drape his arm around her shoulder. She's leaning into him, resting her head on his chest. They look perfect together; they are perfect together.

"As prepared as I'll ever be," I say.

My smile is genuine, but I'm smiling at the two of them, rather than because I am particularly confident about the interview.

"Do you want to go through any more questions?" Zoe asks.

"You've spent long enough helping me," I say. "What I don't know now, I never will."

Two hours we spent, her asking the mock questions and me mumbling through the answers until I could reply without mumbling at all.

"You'll be fine," Luke says. "The interview is just a formality anyway, right? They know you. They know that you can do it."

My mouth feels dry, and I take a gulp of the ice-cold cola. It doesn't help.

"Hey," Zoe says, reading my expression. "Really, you're going to be fine."

"I can't believe I've come this far, to be honest. I don't want to mess it up now."

"I believe it," she says. "And you have come this far despite everything. Despite your anxiety. Despite…"

"That guy," Luke says, interrupting her.

I allow myself a tiny laugh.

"That guy," I repeat. "Yeah, let's just keep it at that."

"He got off lightly. If Zoe ever cheated on me, I don't know what I would do, but we definitely would not be together anymore, and *I* certainly wouldn't be moping around wondering what I had done wrong. She'd be gone. Gone." Luke is resolute, but I doubt he has anything to worry about there.

"Alright, alright. Never going to happen! I shouldn't have even mentioned him," Zoe says. "But you've had a lot to contend with, and still, you have done it. You've completed your course. You got your PAD signed off; you finished all your assignments. You're ready."

I nod. "I hope so."

"Me too," she says. "I'll need you to coach me for my interview next week."

Luke runs his hand along her arm in a supportive rub.

"Zoe Colebrook, soon to be Miss Colebrook, teacher extraordinaire," I smile.

"Unless we get married before she starts work of course," Luke says, without a hint of irony.

Zoe snaps her head around to look at him.

"Just saying," he shrugs.

I would love to say something useful, but instead I make a high-pitched squeaking noise as my excitement slips out.

Zoe looks completely gobsmacked, staring at Luke in a stunned silence.

"Is that a *no* then?" he asks.

"Was that…I mean were you…are you actually serious?" she stammers.

As romantic proposals go, I don't think this would win any awards, but the look on his face tells both of us that he is completely serious.

"Zoe, the past two years with you have been perfect. You are perfect. I never want to be apart from you. Will you be my wife?"

My head is whirring. We're only twenty-one; I can barely hold down a relationship, never mind even think about being with someone forever. Forever is a terribly long time. Still, these two, they are right. They are both perfect, and they are definitely perfect together.

"Luke," she says. "I would love to be Mrs Zoe Buxton. I…yes…yes, I want to be your wife. Yes."

He squeezes her so tightly that I'm afraid

she's going to burst. I give them a good thirty seconds to hug each other before I throw my arms around the two of them, crouching awkwardly behind their chairs.

"I'd better get to be bridesmaid," I laugh.

"That, Violet, is a given," Zoe grins through the happy tears that are streaming down her face.

Chapter Twenty-Nine

I'm too excited about Zoe and Luke to be nervous about the interview. For the first time since I started my placements at St. Jude's I make my way to the Head of Midwives' office on the Margaret Beresford unit. I pop my head into the midwives' staff room, but Geri isn't about today. If everything goes well, if I get through this interview, I'll be back here working alongside her in only a few weeks' time.

It feels unreal. It *is* unreal until I make it happen.

After the interview I walk back to Tangiers Court. I want some time on my own to think about how it went, and how the past three years have gone.

I channelled everything that I've learned over the past three years into that interview. Not only the theoretical knowledge that I gained in lectures or the clinical experience that I have begun to build on my placements, but more than that. I have grown as a person and developed in ways that I could never have imagined. Part of that is growing older.

I have gone from a fresh eighteen-year-old school leaver to a twenty-one-year old future midwife.

I've doubted myself, I've doubted my ability as a girlfriend, but worst of all I have doubted my friendship with Zoe. Now, if I didn't make a complete mess of today, I am going to be starting my dream job, and I know that Zoe will be there by my side, on my side, always.

As for that guy, I'm trying not to think about him. I don't want to give him the headspace. He doesn't deserve it. I was vulnerable and convenient. What does that make him? Whatever it is, I am far better off without him in my life. I wasn't bothered about looking for a boyfriend before I met him, and I am not particularly bothered now. I don't want to be with anyone who doesn't make me feel the way Zoe feels with Luke. Their relationship, with all of its banter, and unconditional love and support is an absolute gold standard. I love them both so much.

It's easy to be positive on such a glorious day. It's the beginning of August, and there's not a cloud in the sky. My black dress was perfect for the interview, but now it's absorbing the heat. I want to be at home in the garden with an ice-cold drink and some cooler clothes. I can kick back, read a book, and wait for the phone to ring.

I don't have to wait too long. I've just about had time to change and settle down in the yard with Zoe when my phone starts to buzz. I know it must be from the hospital.

I don't answer straight away, instead I look at Zoe. She nods.

"Go on. This is it. You've got this."

I take a deep breath and click the button to take the call.

"Hello?" My nervous squeak of a voice creeps out of me. I clear my throat. "Violet Cobham."

I listen to the woman on the other end of the phone line. Zoe stares at me, searching for signs of emotion on my face, but I try to keep a deadpan stoniness.

At the end of the call I put my phone down and look at her.

"Don't do this to me!" she says. "You got it, didn't you? Tell me that you got it."

I can't hold back any longer. My straight face cracks into a wide grin.

"I got it. Zoe, they want me. I'm going to work at St. Jude's. I'm going to be a midwife!"

She grabs me, almost too enthusiastically, and we tumble back on the sofa, squealing and laughing like over-excited children.

"I never doubted it," she finally says, as we calm ourselves enough to sit.

"I doubted myself," I say.

"I never doubted you." The laughter is gone now, and all I feel is the support and love that flows out of her.

"So, this is it," I say. "The end of three years. The end of Tangiers Court."

"This is the beginning," she smiles. "Violet Cobham, midwife."

"Zoe *Buxton*, teacher," I say, placing the emphasis on what will be her new surname.

"Zoe Buxton, wife." She says the words with a smile, but then her face becomes stony serious.

We look at each other in silence, taking everything in.

"You're right," I say. "This is the beginning."

Dear Reader,

Thank you for reading **"Lessons Learned"**, book three in the **"Lessons of a Student Midwife"** series.

If you have enjoyed this book, please consider leaving a review on Amazon and/or Goodreads. Reviews help readers to discover books, and help authors to find new readers. It would mean a lot to me if you would take a few minutes to leave a review.

This is the final book in the series, but if you want to read more about Violet and Zoe, check out my standalone novel **Ghosted**.

If you would like to find out more about new releases and special offers, including information about the rest of this series, please sign up to my mailing list. I'm currently giving away a free full-length novel to everyone who signs up. Visit **jerowney.com** for details.

Best wishes
J.E. Rowney

www.ingramcontent.com/pod-product-compliance
Lightning Source LLC
Chambersburg PA
CBHW061507120726
48001CB00004B/1252